Season by Season

THE WHEEL OF FIRE

**The *Babylon 5* Library
from Del Rey Books**

Babylon 5: *In the Beginning*

Creating Babylon 5

Season by Season Guides

Signs and Portents

The Coming of Shadows

Point of No Return

No Surrender, No Retreat

The Wheel of Fire

Babylon 5 *Security Manual*

Season by Season

THE WHEEL
OF FIRE

Jane Killick

The Ballantine Publishing Group

New York

A Del Rey® Book
Published by The Ballantine Publishing Group

™ and copyright © 1999 by Warner Bros.

http://www.randomhouse.com/delrey/
http://www.thestation.com

Library of Congress Catalog Card Number: 98-96859

ISBN: 0-345-42451-4

Manufactured in the United States of America

First Edition: April 1999

10 9 8 7 6 5 4 3 2 1

Contents

Acknowledgments

So many people came through with videotapes for me this time around that I must thank them all: Alison "Ali" Hopkins, Dominic May, Vena Pontiac, and Aaron Endo at Warner Bros. (who also kindly let me watch some of them in his office!). Thanks also to Chris O'Shea, who was an absolute lifesaver when my printer broke down at the last minute.

But, of course, this book would not have been possible without the generous comments from the cast and crew who gave their time to speak to me. So heartfelt thanks to them and all the people at Babylonian Productions who were helpful during my visit, especially the overworked but ever-cheerful Joanne Higgins. I would also like to mention Aimee Chaille, who was my point of contact at Warner Bros., and my editors Emma Mann and Verity Willcocks, who all helped the writing of this book run as smoothly as possible.

Last, and not least, thanks to David Bassom for providing initial inspiration.

Looking Back Over Five Years

When *Babylon 5* began, in 1992, many claimed that the series was destined to fail, *Babylon 5* creator J. Michael Straczynski recalls. "The odds against us were considerable. I was saying, 'This is going to be a five-year show, period.' They would say, 'What makes you think you will get five years out of this?' [I'd reply] 'We're on a mission from God, okay?' " [*Starburst,* special 35]

The very achievement of making the show last its full, planned five years has been incredibly important for the people who lived through it. Few shows make it that far—and *Babylon 5* nearly didn't. The threat of cancellation was always hanging over it and nearly destroyed it altogether at the end of the fourth year. It was only pulled back from the brink by a change of network, from Warner Bros.' PTEN consortium to cable channel TNT when the former network collapsed. But the commercial success that kept producers, cast, and crew employed for five years is only a side issue in *Babylon 5*'s achievement. Its main success has been fulfilling the story plan that lay at the heart of the show, its famous "five-year arc."

The phrase "five-year arc" has become so synonymous with the show that it tends to get trotted out in a blasé fashion. But back in 1992, this was a new concept. Some shows, particularly soap operas, used continuous story lines that progressed with each episode and were often planned as much as two years ahead. But no one had attempted a story on such a grand scale, where the plot points introduced in the beginning would continue to play a significant part throughout the show's entire length until it reached a predetermined conclusion. Television is a fickle business where shows can be canceled on a whim without warning, leaving the rest of the story untold. Television audiences themselves can be fickle, flitting from channel to channel, picking up on a program halfway into its season or missing the odd episode, and so finding it difficult to follow an ongoing story. Then there are production considerations, like the risk the story line is going to be wrecked by the lead actor getting run over by a bus or the producers wanting to change direction after judging the response of the audience. But Joe Straczynski had worked out his story in such detail that he had faith it could work, and with his famous "trap doors" for every character, he could keep his story on track no matter what production considerations intervened. No one actually had an unpleasant encounter with a bus, thankfully, but when there was a need to replace Sinclair with Sheridan, and when the actress playing Talia Winters (Andrea Thompson) wanted to leave to pursue other work, the trap doors came into play and the story continued because it was the story that was important.

And it was the story that excited audiences. The idea of a story arc that lasted five years may have sounded daunting to the television industry, but it hooked viewers in a way that few television programs ever achieve. "We were able to tell a story over five years where things were foreshadowed in year one and it paid off in year three, in a medium where often you set things up in the teaser and pay it off two acts later," Joe says. "We extended it by years and the audience follows it and gets it . . . We can say to the television community, 'You're wrong—the viewers are not morons, they're sharp people. If you would teach them and talk to them in a straightforward fashion they will react and come to you.' And they have done that." [*Cult Times*, issue 31]

This fresh approach to storytelling kept people talking about *Babylon 5* down at the pub, over the phone, and on the Internet. Speculation about what was going to happen next, what was the meaning of a certain line of dialogue or a certain scene became more profound precisely because it was all planned out ahead of time. Viewers developed their own theories about everything: *What was Kosh hiding under his encounter suit? Could he be an angel? How did he know so much about the future? Could it be that the Vorlons age backwards? Is his apparently benevolent nature hiding his true dark side?* It was a series that got people involved, made them think, and kept them coming back week after week for the next installment. It was an intricate story in which every detail could have significance, where watching and rewatching the episodes could provide new insight. "We proved we were right, right on the production, right on the story," Joe says. "They said it would never work. Now, of course, *Dark Skies* said they had a five-year arc, the new Roddenberry show [*Earth: Final Conflict*] has a five-year arc—this term has now entered the vernacular. We have created something new. That's a good thing." [*Cult Times*, issue 31]

What was also new for science fiction television was *Babylon 5*'s nod of respect to the tradition of the written genre. For a long time, even into the nineties, science fiction television was regarded as something for kids. It was about rockets, robots, and ray guns, people with silly costumes and annoying whizkids. That's not to denigrate the many excellent series that preceded *Babylon 5*—indeed, some of them such as *Blake's 7* directly influenced it—but that perception continued to exist and be reflected in some of the shows getting on the air. *Babylon 5* broke through that barrier and tapped into an audience that had been brought up on written science fiction. The aliens were real aliens. They may have been limited by the practicalities of a television show in that they had to be played by a human actor—although Kosh was an acknowledgment of that restriction, with his true form hidden under the encounter suit—but they were three-dimensional, with a culture and a philosophy all their own. They walked onto *Babylon 5* with a fully sketched background that gave them a depth and a believability rare in science fiction television. The aliens are not simply a metaphor for a part of human nature—e.g., a "warrior race"—but complex peoples with different facets that are gradually revealed. Moreover, the individuals of these alien races have their own personalities, so both G'Kar and Na'Toth are decisively Narn in the way they behave, but are also characters in their own right.

It is clear that the people behind the show understand science fiction. Not only does *Babylon 5* get the terminology right—even *Star Wars* thought a parsec was a length of time, when it's actually a measurement of distance—it also has respect for the concepts that have developed within the genre over the years. In other shows, telepaths tend to be people who can do clever things with their minds, but in *Babylon 5*, the implications of what it might mean to be telepathic, both to the individual and society, are taken into account. This is a testament partly to the amount of thought put into the framework of *Babylon 5* and partly to the tradition of science fiction literature. The Psi Cop played by Walter Koenig is even named in tribute to Alfred Bester, the author of the seminal telepath novel *The Demolished Man*.

Some of the key people on the show, including Joe Straczynski and producer John Copeland, were fans before they were ever television producers, and it is an enthusiasm that can be seen on the screen. "We brought that passion, our passion for man's exploration of space, our imaginations that were stretched by reading science fiction and fantasy growing up, here to this show," John says. "I know Joe is an avid reader and I think that all translated into this show. This is a thinking person's show, this is a smart show. This is a show that deals with the types of material and things that you normally encounter in books, and that's not the case with most science fiction which is on television, or has been on television, or has been in the movie theater. A lot of them are just shoot-'em-up action adventure stories. I think that folks that read science fiction tend to be brighter, are more thoughtful about things, and you have to deliver that to them if you want them to buy into your show. It has to be a smart and interesting and intelligent show, and I think we've tried to do that here."

The intelligence lies in the nature of the story. Science fiction has often been described as a genre of ideas, and *Babylon 5* always delivered compelling ideas, whether they were in the truth about the Vorlons and/or in Sinclair's destiny to become Valen. They stretched the mind and resonated in today's world. If *Babylon 5* has achieved its aim in telling a great story, then it has also said something to its audience along the way. Joe Straczynski said he wanted to show that choices have consequences that bring responsibilities, and that theme is explored over and over again. The most demonstrative example of this is probably Londo's story. He hoped his alliance with the Shadows would return the Centauri to greatness, but it only took them into a war that threatened his Homeworld and eventually pulled Londo down with it, to face his responsibility as an aging, ailing emperor of a ravaged people. If you want to sit back and enjoy the adventure, that is fine, but if you want to look deeper there are other issues to consider.

One of the things that science fiction does so well is comment on the present day at one remove, whether that comment be about racism and the benefits of working together, or about the realities of war. It also shows there are no easy answers. Where a traditional television episode might end on a moral high note with a pat answer to a problem, *Babylon 5* presents an issue in shades of grey, where there is not always a right answer. One early example is Season One's "Believers," where Franklin must decide whether to save a child against his religious beliefs or let him die. "That's the wonderful thing about doing a story that is set in the future," John Copeland says. "That is something that is done again and again in great works of science fiction. They pose the same moral dilemmas and deal with issues that you're able to look at from a different perspective and it's not sucked into your culture with your nationality wrapped around it. In some ways they [the stories] are extremely moral and other ways they are frustratingly amoral because they become much more like life that way. It's not 'good' or 'bad,' it's grey, and endings don't always necessarily become happy endings, they're just endings. It's like everybody wants to have a happy life—well, you don't, you just have a life."

Babylon 5 has never been afraid to reach a new level of storytelling, whether by breaking the simplistic view that the villains are always the villains and the good guys are always straight or true, or by the unconventional use of flash-forwards. *Babylon 5* has been bold and brave with its storytelling, and if one or two elements failed to hit their mark, they are far overshadowed by its successes. The old adage that a story must have a beginning, a middle, and an end, but not necessarily in that order, certainly applies here. In the early days when the show was working hard to set up its complex world, there were hints and visions—"Signs and Portents"—of the great arc that was developing in the background. Later, when the elements of the story were coming together, hints of the future served to intensify the arc. The supreme example of this is "War without End," when Sheridan is thrust forward in time to Centauri Prime where he is a prisoner and Londo is emperor of the devastated planet. Suddenly a whole new set of questions is displayed before the audience.

And then there are the characters. Perhaps it is obvious to say that a drama without good characterization is not dramatic at all, but that has been a flaw of many a science fiction project and television adventure show in the past. In *Babylon 5*, the people are just as important as the plot—they are affected by the plot, and the plot affects them, until the two are so interwoven that one is part of the other. Each person is vividly drawn, from Londo's characteristic quirk of turning a statement into a rhetorical question—as in, "your recent alliance with Mr. Morden, yes?" to Refa in "Ceremonies of Light and Dark"—to Garibaldi's troubled, alcoholic past. The characters also progress in a way that is rare in television. In a normal episodic television show, where the characters begin at the start of the episode is where they have to end at the end of it. The whole format of an episodic show, designed to appeal to the casual viewer, dictates that to be the case. But with *Babylon 5*, the arc of the show is also the arc of the characters. They progress, they learn, and they are affected by what happens around them. Two characters, Delenn and Sinclair, even change species! It is the essence of storytelling for novels, plays, and films, but has never traditionally been the resolve of television. The characters in *Babylon 5* are vivid, complex, and encourage the audience to take the journey with them. Without such effective characterization, the show would lack much of the depth that is its hallmark.

Babylon 5 has become a landmark in science fiction tele-vision, through its approach to both story and production. It was one of the main players in the science fiction boom of the mid-1990s and proved that there was a market out there for intelligent science fiction. For John Copeland, who had spent years trying to sell different science fiction shows to TV networks with fellow producer Douglas Netter, it has been a truly satisfying experience. "What *Babylon 5* achieved is to really put a point on the end of the sentence that there is an audience worldwide for science fiction televi-sion programming that is not *Star Trek*," he says. "For the longest time they all thought in the executive suites that *Star Trek* was its own unique phenomenon. I think as a result of *B5* coming on the air, it has made it possible for shows like *Space: Above and Beyond* and for things like *Sliders*. We've helped pave the way, along with *The X-Files*."

Babylon 5's use of special effects has been another one of its achievements. One of the reasons why television net-works were skeptical of putting money into science fiction was that they knew how expensive it was to generate spe-cial effects. *Babylon 5* came in with a new approach, using computer graphics (CGI). It was uncharted territory, and even the man who spearheaded *B5*'s CGI look, Ron Thornton, secretly wasn't entirely sure how he was going to do it. But the result gave a unique look to the series, and the new technique enabled them to do the sort of shots that would have been impossible with traditional model work. Now everyone's doing it. "The thing that has been done with *Babylon 5* is to say that you can look at new ways of doing things and be successful," John Copeland says. "There were many people who said, 'Oh you're going to do all computer effects and it's not going to work, it's going to be terrible.' Now you look at *Space: Above and Beyond*, which came along two years after us, and they tried to go down the exact same road as we did with all digital effects. I think we have shown that these technologies are embraceable for televi-sion, that you can manage them within the restraints of a television budget and within a television schedule."

But, in the end, the success of *Babylon 5* will be measured by the story it told. "I wanted to create a myth for television on the scale of the *Lord of the Rings* books or the *Foundation* books," Joe Straczynski says, and after five years, that was what he had done. It was a large-canvas story that looked back as far as the first sentient beings in the galaxy, followed mankind into a new age, and looked forward to the destruction of the Earth and humanity's transition into a higher form. It spanned alien races with different philosophies, different cultures, and different faces. It saw characters die, be resurrected, fall in love, be betrayed, and fulfill their destiny. The story gave us the Babylon 5 station, which began as our last, best hope for peace; became our last, best hope for victory; then rose from the ashes of a war to head the push for stability and a new Interstellar Alliance. It is a story that is not entirely over because there will be spinoffs, but it is a story that has been concluded. Perhaps one should leave the last word to its creator, J. Michael Straczynski.

After completing the final-ever episode of *Babylon* 5, "Sleeping in Light," he told fans: "I think . . . people will look back at the whole story, through all these long years and say 'It was a good story' and close the cover and put it on the shelf with the other books . . . and turn off the lights and go to bed feeling that the time was well spent. Which is the most any writer can ever ask for. To tell a tale worth telling, to make people cry, to make people laugh. And even, once in a while, make them think about things and see the world just a little differently than when they began.

"Everything I set out to say, I said. I've carried this story like a hermit crab carries its shell for six long years, counting the pilot. It's been an awfully long and difficult road, and no one will ever really know just how hard the show was to make. Nor should they, because it isn't the difficulty that makes the story, the *story* makes the story. But one way or another . . . when it airs, the burden is off at last. Then it no longer belongs to me. It belongs to you. As it should be. And, in the end, I think you'll be pleased."

"It's these people. I've worked with them a long time, they're like your family and you see them all the time, and

that will be the hardest stuff to leave behind. I won't miss Londo, Londo got to play it out, he found his way to the throne, but I will miss the people."
—Peter Jurasik, Londo

"I've experienced tremendous growth as an actor. I don't even think you can find that in the theater because you never stay with a character long enough. A play is only two hours, but we've had one hundred and ten hours—what a chance to really get into a character and take it through every situation, every twist and turn. So I am just totally grateful for this experience."
—Andreas Katsulas, G'Kar

"I think in the long run *Babylon 5* will be looked at and remembered as one of the very best—if not *the* best— television science fiction series ever made. I'm very proud to be a part of it."
—Bill Mumy, Lennier

"When I first came on the show I had three lines and I turned down two other jobs to do the show because I just really wanted to do it. It was like walking into a comic book. That whole first year was kind of like a mystical experience for me. Every time they called me to come to work, I'd get so thrilled and excited, and I'd turn down other work at times to do the show. This is so much fun to put on this uniform and be a space cop. Man, this is like a dream come true!"
—Jeff Conaway, Zack

"Most important of all has been making friends; good, long-term, solid friends. I love coming to work every day. We have a really close group here and even though we all got into it knowing it was a five-year arc, it's still very sad to see a family break up. No matter where I go I'm always going to take the energy and enthusiasm and the camaraderie of this set with me."
—Jerry Doyle, Garibaldi

"It's been an incredible journey. In Blackpool they've got this big old roller coaster and everyone had to ride it. When you come off, you encourage all your friends 'You gotta go ride the big one.' *Babylon 5*'s the big one and everyone's been telling their friends 'You gotta watch it,' so slowly but surely we're gaining popularity. It's been an amazing ride."
—Patricia Tallman, Lyta

"I think I'll remember the five years I was on *Babylon 5* as being part of a phenomenon, of a science fiction chapter that will go down as, I think, a positive addition to the science fiction television genre. I am lucky enough and fortunate enough to be part of that, and that brings a smile to my face."
—Richard Biggs, Franklin

"I get very attached to my job and my work and I'm sad that it's ending. The highlights for me are, number one, getting the chance to direct, number two, to be involved in such a wonderfully rich show, and number three, making friends."
—Stephen Furst, Vir

"It's been a wonderful experience for me. Joe wrote beautiful stuff for me that really touched me and moved me and had so much to do with my own experience. I agree with him so much, and sometimes I think he wrote it exclusively for me."
—Mira Furlan, Delenn

"This has been the greatest. I am very sad that it's over. I'm very proud to have been on it. This was a great place, a great bunch of people to work with, and you don't get that very often. In my twenty-seven years as a professional actor, this is one of the good ones that I will remember."
—Bruce Boxleitner, Sheridan

Babylon 5's Fifth Season

It had been a hard struggle to get a commission for a fifth and final season of *Babylon 5*. The previous year had been full of uncertainties, with the prospect of cancellation looming so large that portions of the story were slipped into the fourth season to bring the series to a satisfactory conclusion. It was a wise move, had Warner Bros. declared themselves unwilling to stump up the money for more episodes. With the collapse of PTEN, the show had to find a new venue to survive. U.S. cable channel TNT eventually came through at the eleventh hour, having previously obtained the rights to show the first four seasons. This secured a dedicated home for the show and greater exposure in its home country. But after the celebrations died down, one question remained: With some elements of the story moved up into the fourth year, could there really be more story to tell?

The creative force behind the series, writer and executive producer J. Michael Straczynski, had prepared for this moment. In squeezing what story he could into the fourth year, he always knew it was possible that the powers that be would come to their senses and let him have the fifth season he so desired. The remaining story elements planned for Season Five were still untouched. Most obviously, these included the increasing tensions between telepaths and normals—or "mundanes" as they increasingly became known during the fifth season—set up during the preceding seasons, the creation of the new Interstellar Alliance, and Londo's final descent into darkness. After Season Four's frantic pace, the hope was that Season Five was going to be slower and more reflective.

The main arcs for Season Five are the telepath struggle, Londo's rise to power, the bumpy first year of Sheridan's presidency, and the Drakh war. The trouble between telepaths and normals had been building for some time—Lyta had predicted it back in Season Four, and "The Deconstruction of Falling Stars" confirmed that one day there would be a war between telepaths and normals. It is a powder keg waiting to explode, and the spark arrives on Babylon 5 in the shape of Byron. He, himself, is a nonviolent, almost religious figure, but the tension between the two species of humanity is too much to contain even for him. Normals fear telepaths, a fear that has traditionally been tempered by forcing them to join the Psi Corps where they are bound by rules that protect the ordinary citizen. But rogues present a different face: a group of people with extra powers, free to use those powers at their whim. The response to Byron and his followers is inevitable.

This is the type of situation *Babylon 5* handles so well, a dilemma where there is no black and white, and no clear solution that can produce a happy ending for all sides. The Psi Corps, as we have seen, can be an oppressive organization and the rogues only want a place to stay and hide from repression. Making a home on Babylon 5 is not easy, and they are immediately confronted with ignorance and prejudice from the bully boys—or "bad guy types," as the scripts often refer to them—in Down Below. In such circumstances, who could fail to sympathize with the rogues, especially when they have such a charismatic, eloquent leader as Byron? He may borrow some of his nice words from the great writers of history, but the words are powerful, enough to command loyalty from the others and draw in Lyta.

Lyta has come to the stage where she has closed herself off to emotion. She risked herself to try to find Sheridan when he fell at Z'ha'dum, she was an important asset during the Shadow War and instrumental in the final battle in Earth's civil war, but still she found little comfort in the non-telepaths she helped. She was forced back into the Psi Corps to survive, and it is not surprising that she tells Byron, "I don't let anybody in anymore." But gradually she's drawn to his charm, finding hope in his philosophy and love for someone who truly cares for her, not for her powers. Finally, she is able to let someone in, in the most intimate way possible, not only sharing her body with him, but also taking down the barriers in her mind, opening a window to the secrets she had been hiding. This sex scene is one of the most enduring images of the season and something uncharacteristic for *Babylon 5*. It reveals to Byron and his followers that the Vorlons were responsible for creating telepaths and sets the scene for confrontation and tragedy.

Byron has good reason to ask for a Homeworld for telepaths and, on the surface, it would seem to be an acceptable solution to the tensions that have grown up between telepaths and normals. But there is a fatal flaw in his argument. He sincerely believes that telepaths are better than normals, that violence is not their way. But the truth is that evolution may have given them extra talents, but it has not divorced them from human nature. Desperation leads a group of them to respond to their human instincts and turn to violence. From that moment, Byron's cause is doomed. Captain Lochley, left with a hostage situation on her hands, does the only thing she can do to stop the station being held to ransom by terrorists—she calls in Bester and the Psi Cops. It brings the situation to an ugly end. Byron destroys himself, putting an end to the trouble for the moment, but ensuring that his name and his cause live on. He, as Zack predicted the moment he stepped onto the station, has become a martyr. And there *Babylon 5* leaves the telepath situation. Its influence lives on, of course, in Lyta, in her hardened determination to achieve a Homeworld for her people.

Then comes the Drakh war—not so much a war; more of a diplomatic crisis for the new Interstellar Alliance, driven by a series of terrorist-like attacks. The characteristic way *Babylon 5* builds seemingly small incidents into something potentially devastating is equally effective here. The end of the fourth season left the audience with a sense of closure, and although some matters were left unresolved, it was a satisfactory ending. In bringing the story back up to speed again and introducing new threads, *Babylon 5* asks the audience to be patient.

This same trick was used in the first and second seasons, where the series was starting with a blank slate. All was discovery and mystery. The questions What was the hole in

Sinclair's mind? Why was Sheridan's destiny so important? What was the Vorlons' secret agenda? What were the Minbari hiding? continued to nag at the audience while events were building into something more significant. The audience was taken on a journey of discovery, learning about the world of *Babylon 5*, the new alien races not seen before, the characters that lived on the station, and the politics of Earth and the Psi Corps. By the fifth season, much of this material has been explored. The mysteries of the Vorlons and the Shadows are gone, and there is only their legacy to deal with. So something that to Byron and his telepaths is a revelation—that Vorlons created human telepaths—is already known to the audience.

Nonetheless, there is a new struggle to be faced by the members of the Interstellar Alliance, keeping the peace while suspicion and doubt threaten to destroy what they have worked for. Never has Babylon 5 been so much akin to the United Nations as here. The individual races have their own interests to think about, vying for power in a competitive galaxy, with Sheridan in the middle trying to hold it all together. So one attack here, another attack there, with a little misleading evidence to stir the pot, is exactly what is needed to bring the races into conflict. The fragile peace is on the verge of breaking up, barely a year after telling the Shadows and the Vorlons to get the hell out of our galaxy. It is all nicely plotted over several episodes, building small attacks that appear to be the work of Raiders into something more sinister, a concerted effort to destabilize the Alliance. But these maneuverings are not where the drama lies—the drama lies in how they affect the people caught up in them. Indeed, any mystery about who is behind the attacks is deliberately removed by indicating to the audience early on that it is the Centauri. That is important because it focuses attention on Londo. We, as an audience, know exactly what is going on, while he can only suspect something is amiss. We watch helplessly as Londo becomes increasingly isolated by the other races, with evidence steadily mounting against his people. When he finally comes to realize the truth, it is too late to prevent his Homeworld from being bombed and himself from becoming the instrument of the Drakh.

These are the best moments in the season and there are many of them in the final clutch of episodes: Garibaldi's alcoholism being discovered, Delenn and Lennier facing death on a White Star, and the emergence of Lyta's extraordinary powers. They are the payoffs that simply wouldn't have been possible without the setup.

The gentler pace that pervades most of the season is a change in style for the show. J. Michael Straczynski, executive producer and the writer of all but one of the episodes this year, admits that this was his year to experiment. Episodes such as "A View from the Gallery" and sequences like Lyta and Byron making love certainly reflect that. The approach, although different from what has gone before, follows a pattern set up by the preceding seasons, each one with its own identity. Season One was more episodic, Season Two brought the arc into prominence, Season Three was Babylon 5 fighting back, and Season Four was *fast*. The tamer pace of Season Five allows the series to explore the consequences of the previous year and makes room for several stand-alone episodes. Some were more successful than others, with "A View from the Gallery," "The Very Long Night of Londo Mollari," and "Day of the Dead" ranking on most people's favorites list. Focusing on specific subsets of the B5 universe, "The Corps Is Mother, the Corps Is Father" delves a little deeper into the Psi Corps, and "Learning Curve" takes the opportunity to look closer at Ranger training. "A View from the Gallery" is a refreshing episode from the point of view of two maintenance men who not only entertain with their engaging banter, but also provide time for reflection as one of them wonders what it might be like to pilot a Starfury in the heat of battle. "Day of the Dead" is both chilling and moving, giving Londo a final glimpse of happiness with the brief return of Adira and an emotional insight into Lochley's past.

It is the character stories that dominate the fifth year, and no two characters are more engaging than Londo and G'Kar. The history of conflict between their two peoples, their personal histories with each other, and the performances of Peter Jurasik and Andreas Katsulas always produce fireworks. They ended Season Four with a sense of reconciliation, sharing a joke together after Sheridan and Delenn's marriage, but not all issues between them had been resolved.

The issues begin to be addressed in the second episode, "The Very Long Night of Londo Mollari," when Londo, through a series of experiences that force him to face up to his own guilt, genuinely and sincerely apologizes to G'Kar. It clears the air between them, and although G'Kar is not quite prepared to forgive his former enemy, he is able to accept his apology. Their relationship becomes more easy from here on in, described quite succinctly by one of the maintenance men in "A View from the Gallery" as akin to that of a married couple. It is circumstances rather than choice or design that has brought them together, and the continual friction between them is both funny and sad. Peter Jurasik, who plays Londo, aptly describes them as the Odd Couple, bickering away with the banter of a well-rehearsed comedy partnership.

G'Kar becoming Londo's bodyguard keeps them together through some difficult times and allows the relationship to develop further. These two former enemies now have to rely on each other for safety in the Centauri palace. With the discovery of Na'Toth on Centauri Prime and Londo's help in rescuing her, Londo takes the first step toward redeeming himself in G'Kar's eyes. Then, finally, as his planet is being bombed, Londo risks himself to rescue G'Kar from his collapsing jail cell, and G'Kar is brought to a point where he can forgive him.

This final moment between these two is what the whole season had been building toward from their point of view and is one of the most powerful moments they have shared. It is their last good-bye, made all the stronger because of the history that both of them bring to this scene. And lying beneath it is the subtext of Londo's last moments as a free man. He cannot tell anyone, not even G'Kar, about the fate that awaits him. All he can do is hint, which only compounds the sadness for the character. He has done terrible things in a misguided attempt to see his people become powerful again. He has tried to redeem himself and now his greatest enemy is prepared to forgive him, but there is no escaping the consequences for Londo. He knows that he is descending down a dark road, he can see what awaits him at the end of it, yet he has no choice but to follow.

Londo's arc has been one of the strongest throughout the series, following his progression from the drinking, gambling clown he was at the beginning to the lonely emperor he becomes at the end. As the fifth season opens, he knows his destiny is to become emperor, but he cannot know the sorry circumstances that will lead him there. There is a moment of happiness for him in "Day of the Dead"—a night of passion and romance with Adira, and a reminder of what might have been had he taken a different path—but it is only a moment. Political movements take him back to Centauri Prime and a palace where a mad, bumbling regent sits on the throne, ready to kill, if necessary, with conspiracies flitting around the seat of power. It is all ugliness that stems from Londo and his earlier mistakes. Morden saw Londo as the right target for the Shadows to use to start a galactic conflict back in Season Two, and their influence still remains. The Drakh merely took over where their masters left off, controlling the regent with a keeper attached to his neck, manipulating events to start another war, and ultimately controlling Londo. The scene of Londo sitting on the throne in the Centauri palace with all the trappings of the emperor, but totally alone and helpless to resist the Drakh, is the epitome of sadness for this character. It is a tragedy of one who was led astray, even though, in the end, he was the instrument of his own downfall.

One character who had to make an impact if she was to survive in the fifth season was Lochley. She had a hard act to follow, coming in as she did to replace Claudia Christian's Ivanova. The introduction of Lochley injected some needed conflict into the mix as the season opened. With other new plot lines needing time to establish themselves after the neat way Season Four had been wrapped up, Lochley helps beef up the early episodes by stirring up suspicion and doubt. The very fact that she is wearing an EarthForce uniform on a station that once declared independence from Earth sets her apart from the others. Her undeclared loyalties rile Garibaldi and produce some great fiery scenes between them. She is undoubtedly a tough, militaristic woman, who, it turns out, was on the "wrong" side during the civil war, but never do we really have cause to dislike her.

The credit for that must go to a combination of the writing and the acting. The writing introduces the suspicion and doubt from the other characters—capitalizing upon, rather than avoiding, a certain audience uneasiness at having to replace Ivanova—but never are we allowed to be carried along by it. Garibaldi is pretty isolated in his views, and although he may complain about her, he doesn't seem to have any real reason to do so. In fact, steadily and surely his doubts are proved wrong. The key scene for this is in "Learning Curve," when Garibaldi challenges Lochley about her loyalties and she admits she was on the other side in the fight against Earth. She gives such a spirited and ultimately reasonable speech about the ethics of being a soldier and it not being her place to tear up a constitution that she swore an oath to protect, that Garibaldi's position looks untenable. She even receives a round of applause from many in the mess hall, isolating his position even further. This conflict is finally resolved after Garibaldi does some snooping in her private files and she is forced to admit that Sheridan trusts her implicitly because they were once married. It is worth noting that the performances go a long way toward selling this concept, with Lochley's rather embarrassed admission to Garibaldi and his amused reaction that results in the quip, "How many wives has he got?"

It is in this scene that we begin to see the softer side of Lochley. She admits to having made the mistake of falling in love with the wrong guy, and this serves to make her more human, more rounded, and a more likeable character. Although it has to be said that a lot of work in getting the audience to accept her had been done by this point. She stepped onboard with a workmanlike attitude and a determination, but also a smile. If the maintenance man's comment to Lochley in "A View from the Gallery," "You're okay in my book," was an attempt to convince the audience to accept Lochley, he was mostly preaching to the converted. However, getting the character accepted is not the only battle. There is also the challenge of doing something interesting with her, and the highlight for Lochley has to be "Day of the Dead." In the brief return of her friend, Zoe, Lochley has to confront her uncomfortable past that led to drug addiction, squalor, and almost death. It is a tremendously emotional episode for her.

After facing such opposition from Garibaldi when she first came onboard, it is ironic that Lochley is the one who becomes instrumental in making him face up to his alcoholism. Garibaldi has always been one of the most vibrant characters in the series. With a disreputable past, an often explosive personality, and a history of alcohol abuse, he is somewhat of a loose cannon. Garibaldi's arc in the fifth season exploits that and the philosophy of *choices, consequences, and responsibilities* that has dominated *Babylon 5*'s storytelling since the first season.

It is significant that Garibaldi's first drink is not taken on the spur of the moment, but clearly after some consideration. He goes shopping, consciously buys a bottle of booze along with a loaf of bread and other provisions, then sits and contemplates his glass before downing it in one. Subconsciously he understands the consequences of returning to the bottle, something that rises to the surface in a stark dream sequence in "Darkness Ascending" in which he imagines himself responsible for the death of his friends and colleagues on a station ravaged by war. Like other hints of the future that have appeared in *Babylon 5*, it is a prophecy enacted by the rest of the season.

Slowly, steadily, Garibaldi's drinking affects one person after another. His long-term friend on the Drazi Homeworld is killed because alcohol kept him asleep when an assassin came to call. He turns up late and unprepared for meetings, and finally his inaction, brought on by drink, drags the whole Alliance into a potentially devastating war. He fails in his responsibilities and that has consequences not only for him, but for the people he cares about.

These consequences produce some charged moments for Garibaldi as he is gradually forced to face up to his own failures. In the early stages there are hints of remorse as he recounts his friend's death in "The Ragged Edge." Later, as the coherent mask he puts on for other people begins to break down, he exposes his weakness in front of a friend, Zack, and then inevitably in front of the Alliance security council. With his secret so undeniably laid bare, he faces the ultimate confrontation with Sheridan. What makes this scene so effective is that it is played on several levels, a moment that touches a range of emotions; anger, sympathy, sorrow, and friendship.

Once Garibaldi has admitted to his problem, the process of healing begins. With a helping hand from Lochley, he is shown that the support systems he needs to recover were always around him. He has Lise, his friends, and a new life waiting for him on Mars. His desperation was understandable, frustrated at not being able to avenge what Bester did to him, put into a position where he was beaten up and almost shot by rogue telepaths, but the bottle was never the answer.

The story arc for Lennier in the fifth season takes him far away from his beginnings as a sheltered graduate of a Minbari temple and confronts his very private feelings for Delenn. His need to join the Rangers, his dedication to his mission, and his final betrayal of Sheridan all stem from his love for the woman he cannot have. Unable to be around her while she is happily married to another, he leaves Babylon 5 and throws himself wholeheartedly into his Ranger training. When she sends him on an important mission, he responds with equal determination, risking his life for the cause because it is so important to her and because she was the one who asked him. All the while, the subtext of his love remains. His final, fatal moment of weakness in which he decides to let Sheridan die after being such a loyal, faithful, and conscientious companion to Delenn is anguishing to watch. But the groundwork had been carefully laid down. His love for Delenn had, if anything, become stronger since his surprise confession to Marcus back in Season Three. It moved to the surface in his emotional farewell to Delenn before leaving for the Rangers and in his vain hope in "Meditations on the Abyss" that Delenn wants to meet him in Down Below for a clandestine romance rather than to send him on a mission. Morden warns him in "Day of the Dead" that he will betray the Anla'shok, and ten episodes later that is exactly what he does. Lennier later explains it was something that "just happened," a moment born out of emotion, not rationality. Wracked with shame and guilt, he takes off into the galaxy alone.

The season ends by scattering the characters to the four winds, in part to set up possible future adventures for *Crusade* and the other planned follow-up projects, and in part to show that the process of growth and change continues. It is a bittersweet ending that brings the characters to rest, but does not ensure a happy resolution for them all. Garibaldi seems to have finally left his problems behind him, Franklin is given a promotion and the chance to follow his interest in xenobiology on Earth, G'Kar and Lyta are setting off on unknown adventures, and Babylon 5 is left in the capable hands of the supporting cast. But Sheridan and Delenn's journey to Minbar to find wedded bliss is overshadowed by Lennier's actions, Londo faces the prospect of growing old alone as the Centauri emperor, and the Drakh are still waiting in the wings to strike at Sheridan's son when he comes of age.

The story concludes with "Sleeping in Light," the finale filmed the previous year. Although it is strange to see Ivanova back, it is difficult to imagine a more fitting end to such a landmark series. It is a mostly happy end for those that survived and an uplifting conclusion to their five-year struggle. The emotion is at its height as Sheridan says his final farewells to Delenn, his friends and colleagues, and the Babylon 5 station, itself. At the end his death evokes a sense of wonder as he journeys beyond the Rim.

The fifth season was a difficult year for *Babylon 5*. Its challenge was to prove to skeptics that there was more story to tell following the events of the first four years. It was a challenge that the series met head-on, and as a result, *Babylon 5* remains one of the best examples of science fiction to have been made for television.

"The Deconstruction of Falling Stars"

Cast

President John Sheridan ....Bruce Boxleitner
Michael Garibaldi ....Jerry Doyle
Delenn ....Mira Furlan
Dr. Stephen Franklin ....Richard Biggs
Captain Elizabeth Lochley ....Tracy Scoggins
Lennier ....Bill Mumy
Vir Cotto ....Stephen Furst
Zack Allan ....Jeff Conaway
Lyta Alexander ....Patricia Tallman
Londo Mollari...Peter Jurasik
G'Kar ....Andreas Katsulas

Guest Stars

Brother Alwyn Macomber ....Roy Brocksmith
Latimere ....Alastair Duncan
Daniel ....Eric Pierpoint
Brother Michael ....Neil Roberts
Henry Ellis ....Rob Elk
Leif Tanner ....Bennet Guillory
Derek Mitchell ....Doug Hale
Sen. Elizabeth Metarie ....Kathleen Lloyd
Man ....David Anthony Smith
Dr. Barbara Tashaki ....Joanne Takahashi
Jim Bitterbaine ....Kenneth Livingston Taylor
Exeter ....Nick Toth

*Confetti showers down on Sheridan and Delenn as they
walk onto Babylon 5 for the first time since their
wedding. Londo looks unhappily at the celebrations
that, on his world, would be for a funeral. "This is a
very bad sign for the future," he says.*

*One hundred years later and historians are analyzing
President Sheridan's actions. They believe many of the
stories surrounding Sheridan and Delenn are pure myth.*

*They say he had a "good PR machine" that covered up
mistakes such as that which precipitated the telepath
war. But their discussion is interrupted by Delenn, now
one hundred forty years old. They look on in awe at the
old woman, her face now haggard and wrinkled. "He
was a good man," she says slowly, but deliberately. "A
kind man who cared about the world even when the
world cared nothing for him."*

*It's five hundred years since Sheridan set up the
Interstellar Alliance, and Earth is at war with itself. One
half wants to break away from the Alliance and has
constructed a holographic representation of Babylon 5,
which it plans to broadcast to the whole of humanity.
Accurate holographic copies of Sheridan, Delenn,
Franklin, and Garibaldi—complete with their memories
and thought patterns—shimmer into existence. They are
made to play out fictional scenarios that discredit the
foundations on which the Alliance was based, but
Garibaldi's hologram suggests to the programmer that
he can offer something better. He was Sheridan's
strategic planner during the war and could offer that
same service in their conflict, too. The programmer says
their plan is to make the first strike against the enemy,
targeting civilian populations to force a surrender.
Garibaldi smiles and reveals their whole conversation
has been broadcast to the enemy. A warning siren wails
as missiles head their way and the programmer runs out
in terror. The missiles hit, obliterating the holographic
creation in a blast of energy.*

*At one thousand years after Babylon 5 the tales of
Sheridan and the Alliance are but legends. Earth has
been decimated by war and its technology destroyed in
the Great Burn of five centuries ago. One young monk
has dedicated his life to rediscovering humanity's lost
knowledge, but is having a crisis of faith. Earth's only
hope lies in the prophecy of Delenn III, who said
Rangers would come from the heavens in the hour of
need, but it has been so long and they have not come.
Brother Alwyn suggests the Rangers might already be*

here, working secretly where those who fear their scientific knowledge will not notice them. The young monk, somewhat reassured, leaves, and Brother Alwyn takes his Ranger costume from the wardrobe. "We will rebuild the Earth," he says to himself, "but this time we will build it better."

One million years later and the Earth's sun is on the brink of death. One man who has elected to stay behind sends all the records of Human history to New Earth by tachyon relay with the words "You will live on, the voices of our ancestors . . . We created the world we think you would have wished for us. Now we leave the cradle for the last time." His Human form turns into energy and enters a suit that resembles one the Vorlons once used. Out in space, the sun explodes in a ball of fire.

In 2262 Sheridan lies in bed with Delenn, wondering if what they did will be remembered in a thousand years' time. She tells him they did what they did because it was right, not to be remembered. "History," she says, "will tend to itself."

"The Deconstruction of Falling Stars" ends with a simple on-screen message: "Dedicated to all the people who predicted that the Babylon Project would fail in its mission. Faith manages."

Babylon 5 set out with a mission to tell a story over five years, and throughout that time people doubted that it could be done. The five-year struggle to sell the series to a television network is proof enough of that, but the greatest uncertainty was during the fourth season. During that time it seemed increasingly likely that Warner Bros. would pull the plug. But at the last minute, a deal was struck to find *Babylon 5* a new home on American cable channel TNT, and the series was saved. "Sleeping in Light" was therefore put aside to be shown at the end of the series proper, and a new episode, "The Deconstruction of Falling Stars," was put in its place to bridge the gap between the fourth and fifth seasons. The very fact that it was made and broadcast was a testament to the lasting power of *Babylon 5* and a signal to those who thought that a fifth season would never happen.

"The Deconstruction of Falling Stars" was the first episode to be made under the new TNT regime and signaled a change to filming an episode in six days rather than the usual seven. The first director to have to cope with this was Stephen Furst, better known to viewers as the actor who plays Vir. "It's tougher," he says, "but nothing is impossible. I'm glad I was able to pull it off. I'm glad there wasn't any director before me that had done it, and I came along not being able to do it." The series finale "Sleeping in Light," however, had previously been shot in six days by freshman director Straczynski.

Jerry Doyle, who, as Garibaldi, had more to do in this episode than any other of the regular cast, agrees that from an actor's point of view it made very little difference. "In the beginning it was a fairly rough transition to bring it up to speed, but now it seems to have found its own groove," he says. "I think it's tougher on the crew and everyone who's building 'em and moving 'em and trying to get the wardrobe ready. We just walk a little faster and talk a little faster, that's pretty much it. I haven't seen a big difference personally. We've got such a large cast that a lot of the stuff gets spread out anyway, so the workload is broken up amongst us all."

The fifth season also has a different style from the previous four, which is seen clearly emerging in "Deconstruction." The monk scene, for example, takes up virtually one whole act, between commercial breaks, and is set in only one room. "This year is more character oriented," writer and executive producer J. Michael Straczynski confirms. "Year four was the year of things going 'boom!' a lot, and I try not to do the same thing twice in a row. Given that . . . you can have more lengthy dialogue which, again, I love anyway and it makes it easier to shoot. It's been fairly straightforward to make the adaptation. It's a higher burden on me because we need scripts every six days, not every seven days, and over the long haul a day here and a day there adds up. So you have twenty-two days less over the course of the season to write." [*TV Zone*, issue 99]

At the beginning of the episode, Sheridan remarks that in a hundred years' time people probably won't remember who they were. His remark is repeatedly disproved as we make the journey through several time periods and see that people remember not only Sheridan and Delenn, but also what they achieved. It is just the interpretation of what they achieved that changes. The three commentators who gather to debate on an ISN program shortly after the foundation of the Interstellar Alliance manipulate the facts to suit their own purposes; the historians who discuss Sheridan and Delenn one hundred years later interpret the events to suit their own arguments. Their giant faux pas is to dismiss stories that Delenn is still alive at one hundred forty years old. When she arrives in the studio unexpectedly, she not only proves them wrong, but also discredits their authority to speak on the subject of her life.

This sequence meant actress Mira Furlan had to sit in the makeup chair for a long time to be transformed into an aged Delenn. "That was a scary thing to do," she says. "I was afraid how it was going to turn out because it was an extreme choice from a writer's and an actor's point of view, one hundred forty. But I was glad to see that it worked in the end and it came out well. I was really satisfied. Somehow it had some reality. I was doubting that anybody would buy it, but it had an emotional aspect that I did not expect. Joe promised that he wouldn't develop the theme of one-hundred-forty-year-old Delenn, and I was glad of that because it's hard to wear that makeup."

The emphasis then changes as the sequences move further into the future. Sheridan, Delenn, and their achievements have become almost legendary. So much so that five hundred years later, a hologram simulation is made to "deconstruct" and discredit them in order to persuade Earth's population to split from the Alliance. Another five hundred years and humanity is living in the aftermath of the resulting war, "the Great Burn," and Sheridan and Delenn's memories are now held in a holy book.

The sequence with the two monks is the favorite part of the episode for director Stephen Furst. "I loved it, it was like doing something that wasn't *Babylon 5*," he says. It was an idea that came to Joe Straczynski while he was researching the English medieval church for another project: "Knowing the role they [monks] played in maintaining secular knowledge from about A.D. 500 and for some time thereafter, that seemed the perfect route to go that would also resonate with the look of the Rangers and the religious Minbari and the whole feel we were setting up."

But as he started to write it, he realized it bore a similarity to *A Canticle for Leibowitz*, Walter M. Miller Jr.'s classic science fiction novel about an order of monks working to preserve knowledge after a nuclear holocaust. "For several days I set it aside and strongly considered dropping it, or changing the venue. At one point [I] considered setting it in the ruins of a university, but I couldn't make that work realistically. Who'd be supporting a university in the ruins of a major war? Who'd have the resources I needed? The church, or what would at least look like the church. My sense of backstory here is that the Anla'shok moved in and started little abbeys all over the place, using the church as cover, but rarely actually a part of it, which was why they had not gotten their recognition and would never get it. Rome probably didn't even know about them, or knew them only distantly. Anyway, at the end of the day, I decided to leave it as it was, since I'd gotten there on an independent road." [*TV Zone*, issue 99]

The two sequences set five hundred and a thousand years into the future show that victory against the Shadows and the Vorlons did not achieve a lasting peace. A depressing thought, perhaps, but a realistic one according to Joe. "No one and nothing will ever solve all of our problems at once, now and forever," he says. "People will always be people. You can't wave a magic wand and fix it all. Yes, there was another war, but had the Shadows not been stopped by our characters, there likely wouldn't have been a human race at *all* anymore. Yes, there was a war and many died in it, as tends to happen in war, but the nominal right side in it came out on top, which would not have been the case but for Garibaldi's simulacra giving them a leg up on things. We have had, continue to have, and will always have wars and grief and struggle, we will climb up and fall down, but each time we climb a little higher and in the end we *do* build the world that our ancestors would have wanted for us. We do leave the cradle at last and we take our place among the stars teaching those who follow us." [*TV Zone*, issue 99]

The final sequence is set one million years into the future, from where, it becomes clear, all the older records were being viewed. Sheridan and Delenn's legacy survived through the Great Burn in the form of the Rangers, who were able to nurture humanity back on the path to a higher state. The man who was viewing the historical records acknowledges his ancestors before his body turns to energy and enters a Vorlon-like encounter suit. The reference is a deliberate one and suggests that Humans have become as powerful as the First Ones. Sheridan and Delenn's Babylon Project did not fail. It endured through aeons of struggle and led to the ultimate ascent of Humankind.

The Wheel of Fire

of Fire

Episode Guide

1
"No Compromises"

Cast

President John Sheridan	Bruce Boxleitner
Michael Garibaldi	Jerry Doyle
Delenn	Mira Furlan
Dr. Stephen Franklin	Richard Biggs
Captain Elizabeth Lochley	Tracy Scoggins
Zack Allan	Jeff Conaway
Londo Mollari	Peter Jurasik
G'Kar	Andreas Katsulas

Guest Stars

David Corwin	Joshua Cox
John Clemens	Anthony Crivello
Byron	Robin Atkin Downes
Simon	Timothy Eyster
Ranger	Mauricio Mendoza
Station Worker	Michael Manzoni

President Sheridan welcomes aboard the new EarthForce officer who is to replace Ivanova. "You have full and complete authority in the running of Babylon 5," he says, extending a hand. Captain Elizabeth Lochley takes it and shakes it firmly.

Lochley walks alone through Brown Sector until out of the shadows comes Byron, an elegant, soft-spoken man and a strong telepath. Behind him emerges his group of telepathic followers, all rogues trying to stay one step ahead of the Psi Corps. Byron introduces her to one of them, a silent boy they call "Special Simon." The boy smiles at Lochley and a magnificent image of flowers fills her mind. Byron says the telepaths mean no harm; all they want is somewhere to stay.

Sheridan glares at the message that has appeared on the monitor in his quarters. "As of today, you are officially a dead man," it reads. The computer then

relays a second message, this time spoken by a man's
voice. "You started the civil war back home, Sheridan.
The people who died are your responsibility. And I'm
here to make sure you pay the price for your actions."
Garibaldi later traces the voice pattern to a Major John
Clemens, a former EarthForce officer under President
Clark.

Clemens stalks through the Alien Sector with a PPG
in his hand. He breaks into the Gaim ambassador's
quarters and, before the alien has a chance to react, cuts
him down with a blast of plasma fire. Clemens takes the
Gaim's atmosphere suit to his quarters, where he works
to conceal a weapon inside it. Beside him a music box
plays a serene tune that drifts through the air ducts.
Simon, the special telepath, is drawn toward the sound
and crawls through the ducts to Clemens' quarters.
What he finds are images of horror—the assassin's
thoughts of raising his gun to Sheridan, firing, and seeing
him grimace in pain. Simon is repulsed and tries to crawl
away, but Clemens hears him and fires his PPG at the
ceiling.

Simon, wounded and bleeding, stumbles into the
Rotunda where Sheridan's inauguration ceremony is
about to take place. Dignitaries scatter as he collapses in
Franklin's arms. Simon looks up to see a "Gaim" rip off
its helmet and reveal Clemens inside. "No!" Simon
screams, and projects images of Sheridan's assassination
into every mind in the room. Security guards fire, but
Clemens grabs a hostage before they can bring him
down and backs out of the room.

Unperturbed, Sheridan and the other dignitaries
gather in the Sanctuary. G'Kar turns to Sheridan to
swear him in, but everyone else in the room is staring
out of the window, where a Starfury hovers dangerously
close. The sound of Clemens' voice reverberates through
the PA system. "Time to pay the piper," he says, and
prepares to fire. A second Starfury with Garibaldi at the
controls appears and grabs hold of Clemens' Starfury

*with a grappling hook. Clemens fires as the two joined
ships spin out of control, missing his chance to destroy
Sheridan. Guns rise from the Babylon 5 defense grid,
and Garibaldi releases the hook and pulls away. The
guns fire and destroy Clemens' Starfury in a ball of fire.*

*Byron enters Sheridan's office where the newly sworn-
in president sits waiting for him. Lochley denied the
telepaths permission to set up a colony on Babylon 5,
but Sheridan has decided this is a political decision that
should come under his authority, not hers. One of
Byron's people saved his life, he says, and for that they
can stay.*

"No Compromises" is the first episode to feature Tracy
Scoggins as the tough, no-nonsense Captain Elizabeth Lochley. Any doubts she could replace Claudia Christian's Ivanova—Claudia, offered the chance to appear in a
TV movie, decided not to sign on for Season Five when her
contract option expired during negotiations to move the show
to TNT—are swept away with Tracy Scoggins' entrance in
the show. She makes an impact from the very first scene and
continues to impress throughout the episode. "I really
wanted the part badly, I would have been inconsolable if I
hadn't got my way," Tracy says. "I like the show and I'd read
interviews about what a happy set it was and [how] it was
self-contained out here and the producers and the writers
were accessible and concerned themselves with things that
matter, as opposed to people on the lot at some other studio who are worried about having the best parking spot. I
wanted to be part of this family."

Lochley was obviously a big role with the potential to play
a large part in Babylon 5's future and casting the right
person was key. Jerry Doyle was brought in to read at the
auditions alongside the final five women up for the part. He
was told to give it his best shot to see if the potential
Lochleys could stand up to him. "At the end of my first audi-
tion with him Lochley wins the scene, so to speak," Tracy
remembers. "As I finish my last word he goes, 'Oh bite me.' I

turned to him and said, 'Lick me twice, all right?' This is in front of a room full of executives and people I don't really know, but I just wasn't about to take that and Lochley wouldn't take it either. Then the next time he made some remark I said, 'Mr. Garibaldi, I'm afraid I'm going to have to ask you to kiss my ass,' and I walked out of the room." After that, Jerry Doyle turned to the producers and announced, "She's the one."

"It's a fun set and that's the kind of stuff that goes on here all the time and I knew that, for me, she was it," Jerry says. "In addition to that, her performances got stronger in each scene in the call backs. Actingwise, it was the clear choice. But also personalitywise it was right on the money for me and I said, 'Guys, that's the one.' "

The injection of Lochley into the status quo helped shake things up, just like when Sheridan replaced Sinclair back in the second season. "Storywise it's given us a little conflict we didn't have at the end of Season Four," writer and executive producer Joe Straczynski says. "Things had more or less worked out by that point, everyone was on speaking terms with everyone else, and having someone whose loyalties are uncertain gives us some conflict. Our cast consists mainly of rebels and smart-asses and she fitted right in with that. She's a pistol and she gets on with everyone because of that—it's not a case of a shrinking violet." [*Starburst*, special 35]

With such a strong and important character, it was essential that Lochley make an impact right from the beginning. Director Janet Greek remembers that was one of her priorities on this episode. "Joe and I talked quite a lot about her character and what he wanted to see, and I worked with Tracy quite a lot," she says. "She's very talented and she came in with a lot of preparation as well, and then we just worked really hard on the set to make sure, to mold that character so it would be what Joe had in mind. I think Tracy did a really good job on that first episode."

She was not eased into the show, either, but thrown in at the deep end. "My first day I was in every scene and had a trainload of dialogue," Tracy remembers. "But everyone went out of the way to make everything work well and make me very much not the new kid on the block."

No sooner has Lochley arrived at the station than she is faced with her first tough decision. A group of telepaths, led by the enchanting and enigmatic Byron, arrives seeking sanctuary on the station. "I see him as a man who is extremely passionate about his people," Robin Atkin Downes, the British-born actor who plays Byron, says. "He is someone who's trying to create a change and put an end to the oppression. To me, he's like Martin Luther King, I see him as having the potential to be a great leader. When we see him he's just starting, gathering the people together, gathering them on the hill, so to speak. He's somebody who has a dream for something better, he's somebody who's obviously had a disturbing background. Something has driven him to pursue this endeavor."

Byron's arrival sets up trouble for the future, and everyone, it seems, knows it. Zack senses the hint of the martyr in Byron's attitude, Lochley knows it and refuses the rogues permission to stay, and even Sheridan, who reverses Lochley's decision, acknowledges that a telepath war is coming. This is just one of a number of plot threads that are set up in this episode, awaiting future development. Lochley's arrival sets up a conflict with Garibaldi, and hints at a certain uneasiness with Sheridan, while the attempt on Sheridan's life reveals the opposition that he and the new Alliance will face over the coming year. It is somewhat of an introductory episode, bringing in not only new elements like Byron and Lochley, but also reacquainting audiences with the situation on *Babylon 5*. This was a deliberate ploy by Joe Straczynski, who realized that the show's new U.S. home on the TNT cable channel would bring with it new viewers. "We always start slow each season, especially in this case, knowing that we're going to get a lot of new viewers. I structured the show so it would bring folks up to date ASAP on who everybody is and where things stand."

With so many introductions going on, plus the assassination plot, it was a tough episode for Janet Greek to direct, especially under the new, shortened six-day schedule.

"Everybody worked so hard, the crew were just miraculous on that, they just really pulled together and did a really great job," she says.

Nevertheless, the hard work didn't stop her having a bit of fun. Eagle-eyed viewers will notice the camera lingering on a large bowl of oranges in the first scene after the opening titles, a deliberate nod to the beginning of the second season when Bruce Boxleitner first arrived to play Sheridan. "I directed Bruce's first episode," Janet remembers. "In that episode Joe had him walking around the station talking about oranges all the time. He had an orange in his hand, he was tossing an orange in the air, he was always talking about the fact that he'd never had fresh oranges in space and he was so happy that he could get fresh oranges on B5. So in this episode there was a bowl of oranges in his quarters, there were oranges all over the station—I mean, it was hysterical!"

And if you thought that was the end of the oranges, you'd be wrong. Watch out for those oranges because they'll be back.

2
"The Very Long Night of Londo Mollari"

Cast

President John Sheridan	Bruce Boxleitner
Michael Garibaldi	Jerry Doyle
Delenn	Mira Furlan
Dr. Stephen Franklin	Richard Biggs
Lennier	Bill Mumy
Vir Cotto	Stephen Furst
Zack Allan	Jeff Conaway
Londo Mollari	Peter Jurasik
G'Kar	Andreas Katsulas

Guest Stars

Ruell	Ross Kettle
Med Tech	Akiko Ann Morison
Lord Refa	William Forward
Emperor Cartagia	Wortham Krimmer

"No! No, no, no, no!" Londo rages. "This is completely unacceptable!" Londo picks up a bottle of Brivari liquor from a nearby box and waves it at Zack. Zack is unimpressed—there have been several recent infestations and he has orders to impound all incoming food and drink for three days. Vir takes Zack aside to placate him, leaving Londo to sneak a sip from the bottle. A tightness claws at his chest, he staggers, clutching at the pain. The bottle falls from his hand and smashes to the ground. Vir and Zack rush over to find Londo collapsed on the floor.

Lennier enters Delenn's quarters, fresh with her itinerary for the day. But she is in a somber mood; she has heard that Lennier has decided to leave her side. "You have Sheridan now," he explains. "I'm . . . in the way." He says he is leaving for Minbar to join the

*Rangers, and as he speaks, there are tears in his eyes.
And tears in hers.*

*Delenn and Sheridan stand vigil over Londo, who lies
unconscious in Medlab. Dr. Franklin has done all he
can—the rest, Sheridan reflects, is up to Londo. Delenn
looks down at him. "Good luck, Mollari," she says
softly.*

*Delenn's words—"good luck . . . good luck . . ."—
echo in Londo's thoughts. He is standing in a twisted,
dreamlike version of Down Below. He turns, looking for
Delenn, and is drawn to a curtained area at the end of
the hall. There, Delenn sits at a table, her face shrouded
in a black lace veil. "Do you want to live?" she asks
him. He says—softly, almost afraid of the answer—that
he does. "That is not enough," she tells him. She turns
over a card from a fortune teller's pack to reveal his past.
It is covered in blood.*

*As doctors work frantically on Londo's body in
Medlab, his mind enters darkness where he finds Vir.
"Turn around," Vir tells him. But Londo dares not, he
can feel the one red eye and one blue eye of G'Kar
watching him from behind. "You're out of time, Londo.
Turn around." Londo turns and there is G'Kar, standing
over him.*

*G'Kar retrieves images from Londo's past: Londo
looks on while the Narn Homeworld is bombarded by
the Centauri. "You said nothing!" cries G'Kar. Londo
looks on while G'Kar is whipped for Emperor Cartagia's
pleasure on Centauri Prime. "And you said nothing!"
Then suddenly Londo is in G'Kar's place, being
whipped, while G'Kar sits in Cartagia's place, gleefully
watching the spectacle in front of him. "One word. I
want to hear it," says G'Kar.*

*Back in Medlab Londo's heart arrests and medtechs
rush for the defibrillator. "One! Two! Three!" G'Kar
cries with the strokes of the whip. In Medlab, the
defibrillator shocks electric current through Londo's
heart. "Sixteen! Seventeen! Eighteen!" and Londo's body
jolts on the bed. "Thirty-four! Thirty-five! Thirty-six!"*

His heart is shocked again, but doesn't respond. "Thirty-nine!" And Londo cries out in pain as the final shock of the defibrillator gets his heart beating again.

Londo is back in the darkness with G'Kar, almost all of the strength taken out of him. "Just a word, Mollari. That's all it takes." The floor beneath him is glowing red, pulsating with the weak beating of his heart. Londo pounds the floor, over and over. "I'm sorry," he cries with each punch of his fist. "I'm sorry. I'm sorry."

In Medlab, Londo awakes to see G'Kar watching him discreetly from a distance. He turns his head toward him. "I'm sorry, G'Kar . . . I'm sorry." G'Kar sees Londo's apology is genuine and smiles, tears welling in his eyes.

With Londo's heart attack comes the prospect of death and time for reflection for the man who caused so much suffering through his association with the Shadows. The weight of that knowledge has pressed down on him so hard that the only way he is going to survive is to confront it. "What was really fun about that episode when I look back on it, was so much of it was in dream sequence," Peter Jurasik, who plays Londo, says. "Like the scenes with Bruce where he's sitting at the bar chatting and then Bruce's costume changes throughout the scene, and the gypsy stuff with Mira, those were fun things to do."

The director charged with the task of creating a dreamlike feel for the episode was David Eagle. "When I read the script I realized that a lot of the imagery that was going on was similar in some respects to what we saw in 'Dust to Dust' in Season Three," he says. "I thought we were going to have a lot of this black limbo kind of look, and the script is written very dark so the lighting and even the film exposure would be dark. And talking with Joe and John and [director of photography] John Flinn, that's what we decided. It's a very, very dark show all the way around. Most of the way the script was written called for those strange images and imagery, and there were certain things that really cried out for the audience's reaction to be 'What was *that*?'—they'd look at something and go 'Whoa! What's happening here?' and 'Why is this person dressed that way?' or 'Look at that, his clothes change in every other shot.' I went into it thinking I really have to come up with some very strange looks here because it is a very strange show."

One of those strange looks heralds the second dip into Londo's dream world. It happens in the Zocalo after Vir says good-bye to Lennier and walks down the corridor to the transport tube. The lighting changes as we pass from reality into a dream world, the camera tilts to one side, and Londo walks around the corner. The camera then follows him to the bar of the Zocalo, all in one continuous shot. "We had to get a hundred people off the stage in five seconds," David says. "They not only had to get off the stage quietly and out of sight, but they had to take all the props that they had with them, too. So bottles and glasses and food and plates and all kind of other things had to be cleared off immediately."

The only cut in that shot is a brief close-up of Londo in which his face stays still in the frame while everything else around him changes perspective as he is walking. It was achieved by strapping the camera onto Peter Jurasik so it moved as he moved. "I made them scratch out who the cameraman was," he recalls with a chuckle. "It always says John Flinn's name, so I made them strike out that and put Peter Jurasik as the cameraman for that one slate."

Londo encounters various figures in his dream world, all of them leading to the one person he must ultimately face— G'Kar. Actor Andreas Katsulas was also reminded of Season Three's "Dust to Dust" and took it as another opportunity for G'Kar to touch Londo's mind. "Because G'Kar ultimately is Londo's conscience in one way or another," he says. "I obviously wasn't in his mind, it's more what Londo's thinking that G'Kar might say or that part of Londo is trying to say to himself and does not recognize."

So tortured is Londo with the pain that he put G'Kar and his people through, that his mind puts him in the same position that G'Kar was in while imprisoned in the Centauri palace. In "The Summoning" it was G'Kar who was whipped for the pleasure of the insane emperor. In "The Very Long

Night of Londo Mollari" it is Londo who must face the lashes of the electro-whip. "When we had done the scene the first time, Andreas did it so well," Peter says. "It was harkening back and echoing that stuff, so it was a little daunting to step into the big Narn shoes. But I had a good time, it was really an interesting episode to do."

In the place of Cartagia is G'Kar, with an expression on his face that reflects the mad smile of the former Centauri emperor. "I personally don't have a talent to do impressions, I'm so dreadfully bad at that, but I did have my memory of how it was," Andreas says. "I proceeded from that and didn't look at tapes to get down every gesture and posture and try and find his voice or anything. He had an effeminate quality, I felt, and I just tried to use that."

During this sequence Londo approaches the fortieth lash, which will kill him, while back in the Medlab he goes into cardiac arrest. In the real world, it is Dr. Franklin's use of the defibrillator that gets Londo's heart pumping again, but in Londo's mind it is the scream he gives on the thirty-ninth lash that stops the whipping and pulls him back from death.

When Franklin pulls back Londo's shirt to lay the defibrillator paddles on his chest, it reveals Londo's Centauri genitalia, previously seen only once, cheating at cards in Season One's "The Quality of Mercy." "I'm not an actor who has played a lot of romantic stuff, but I guess it's a little like when you finally get to your romantic scenes and people get giggly and don't quite know what to do with themselves," Peter says. "They arrived with great fanfare—the six tentacles came bobbing onto the set and they were placed ceremoniously on my chest. People were moving them all around, and costume people were giggling and pushing them inside my shirt, and makeup people were patting them down with powder, and they became much more important than me or anybody else in the scene for a while. Also, when we did the takes when Rick Biggs, Doctor Franklin, is supposed to tear open Londo's blouse to reveal them, more than once he tore open the blouse and as he did so got a little tentacle in his hand and yanked one or two of them off!"

The result of all the pain that Londo goes through is some

sort of understanding of the suffering he caused. As G'Kar says, he committed all those acts and said nothing. Now he must rectify that with an apology. It must be a very hard thing to convey so much emotion in only two words, "I'm sorry." "It was a bit," Peter says, "but my fellow actor was Andreas at that point and he was just waltzing around me for three or four minutes berating me, and if I didn't come up with 'I'm sorry' I would have screamed 'Stop!' because he was just laying into me!

"The other thing is the character Londo is dying to release that. He carries that stuff around. He says 'I've never said I'm sorry to anyone.' Well, that's kind of an extraordinary place to find yourself in life, where you've never tasted the sweetness of forgiveness and what that is in life. Talk about deprived! In one of the other episodes where they talk about their childhood, 'A View from the Gallery,' Londo talks about what a deprived childhood he had. And when you say you've never said you're sorry before in your life and mean it, you're speaking of a pretty deprived life. So he's dying to say it. In that sense, when it comes out, it's something he really wants to release. For Peter the actor, it was fun to do. These high dramatic moments, these arching moments are great."

The apology finally settles the unspoken business between G'Kar and Londo, paving the way for the closer relationship, almost a friendship, that builds through the fifth season. But it does not and cannot redeem Londo entirely. "He can learn, yes, and he can better himself," Joe Straczynski argues, "but because of his actions, so many have died, so much grief has occurred, that perhaps no amount of self-revelation can cover the blood on the floor." And, as flash-forwards to Londo's time as emperor have already shown, he will continue to pay for what he has done right up until his death at G'Kar's hands.

The subplot in this episode involves Lennier's decision to leave Delenn and join the Rangers. The scene in which he explains his reasons is really quite a touching one, full of subtext and emotion. As we shall see, it is a subtext that will come to prominence and shape Lennier's fate as the season progresses. "I've had some really wonderful moments with

Mira over the course of this project and as I recall that was one of the more intense," actor Bill Mumy says. "The understanding of telling her I loved her without saying it, was what we were trying to convey. I think Delenn knew and Lennier certainly didn't have the courage to tell her. I liked that and I was happy that he's gone off to be a Ranger. Rangers are cool. I am 'the Bone Ranger—only a White Star away'!"

3
"The Paragon of Animals"

Cast

President John Sheridan	Bruce Boxleitner
Michael Garibaldi	Jerry Doyle
Delenn	Mira Furlan
Dr. Stephen Franklin	Richard Biggs
Zack Allan	Jeff Conaway
Lyta Alexander	Patricia Tallman
Londo Mollari	Peter Jurasik
G'Kar	Andreas Katsulas

Guest Stars

Verchan	Tony Abatemarco
Byron	Robin Atkin Downes
Drazi Ambassador	Kim Strauss
Merkat	Daniel Bryan Cartmell
Ranger	Bart Johnson

Garibaldi walks down a darkened corridor in Brown Sector, thinking about the proposition he is about to put to Byron, the leader of the rogue telepaths living in Down Below. He thinks the Interstellar Alliance should employ telepaths to gather covert information, but his thoughts precede him, loud enough for Byron and every other telepath to hear even before he opens his mouth. "The answer is no," Byron tells him flatly.

In Medlab, a Ranger lies fatally injured, the information he tried so hard to bring to the station locked within his unconscious mind. Lyta puts her hand on his forehead and scans him. She sees a memory of a group of people—the Enfili—huddled around a fire telling of the Raiders that have decimated their world. Then Lyta looks up to see the specter of the Ranger standing at his own bedside. "I'm dying, aren't I?" he

says. Lyta nods and watches him as he turns toward a
whirlpool of light that has appeared in the wall and
steps through. Suddenly, he is gone, and Lyta is pulled
back to reality. She later tells Garibaldi that being inside
his mind when he died made part of her go cold. "It
pulls you in," she says, "and a little piece of your soul
goes with him."

Sheridan decides to send the entire White Star fleet to
the Enfili Homeworld as a message that the Alliance will
not tolerate one group of people victimizing another.
The Enfili planet lies on the outskirts of Drazi space, so
Sheridan asks the Drazi ambassador for help and they
agree that their two fleets will first meet at a rendezvous
point. When the ambassador leaves the meeting, he
passes close to Byron in the corridor, and the Drazi's
thoughts stray into Byron's telepathic mind.

Lyta goes to see Byron on Garibaldi's behalf. He pulls
out a chair and tells her to sit. She takes a couple of
steps forward, but he kicks the chair away from her. "It
was not phrased as a request, now was it?" he says.
"Has it occurred to you that you deserve better?" He
then asks her politely to sit down and she does,
somewhat wary, but intrigued by him. "That's why
we're here," he tells her. "Because we're tired of being
ordered around by those who cannot hear the song we
hear." She warms to his gentleness, but when he reaches
out a hand to touch her face, she pulls away. Byron
returns to the business at hand and says that if it matters
to her, he will agree to help Garibaldi.

Lyta tells Sheridan the thoughts that Byron picked up
from the Drazi ambassador. The Raiders are in league
with the Drazi, preying on worlds like the Enfili's and
sharing their spoils. The Drazi plan to wipe out the
entire Enfili Homeworld before the White Star fleet
arrives.

Sheridan tells the ambassadors of the Alliance that the
White Stars are proceeding straight to Enfili to
annihilate the entire fleet of Raiders believed to be about
to attack. The Drazi ambassador has to admit that the

White Stars will be destroying Drazi, not Raider ships,
and begs to be allowed to warn his government to stop
his people from being killed. Sheridan allows him to run
to a StellarCom, then turns to the other ambassadors.
This one incident, he says, shows how important it is for
them all to sign a declaration of principles. G'Kar hands
out scrolls to all of those present. Quietly and peacefully,
the ambassadors of all the races represented in the room
take a pen and put their signatures to a common cause.

The title "The Paragon of Animals" is taken from Shakespeare's *Hamlet*, and, unusually for *Babylon 5*, that reference is pointed up when Byron quotes almost the entire speech when he first meets Lyta. The words in their original context are a celebration of mankind and all its abilities, but for Byron they are a display of man's ego. When Hamlet spoke those words he was delighting in man's nature, but when Byron says them he is being ironic. "One of the wonderful aspects of Shakespeare's work is that it lends itself to reinterpretation and reinvention," Joe Straczynski comments. "Cynical lines can be read with hope, and vice versa."

To borrow such language to make a point is exactly in character for Byron, a man whose very name echoes the classical poets. "Joe has just written some amazing poetic language for Byron," actor Robin Atkin Downes says. "He's very classical, very lyrical, and I love the classic. I love Shakespeare, I love that he's given Byron Shakespeare quotes and he flashes into poetry every once in a while. I love how passionate the character is, and I love that he wears his heart on his sleeve. It's such a juicy role to play."

Robin started acting professionally in the theater at the age of seventeen and only began film and TV work three years before being cast as Byron. Although that training helped with the theatrical nature of the show, it was not something he wanted to bring to the classic speeches he had on *Babylon 5*. "I don't want people to look at my work and say 'What a grandiose theater man he is' because I don't think you see that when you watch Patrick Stewart or other people who have worked on the stage. I believe as an actor that you can be bigger than life, but as long as it's based in reality no choice can be too strong. Those are the actors that excite me when I watch the movies, [the ones] that make strong choices."

Byron uses Hamlet's speech to make a point and it is a performance that is leveled entirely at Lyta. There is almost a sense of seduction in the way he talks to her and touches her cheek. Most of the moves come from him, but there is clearly an attraction there, even if Lyta is not quite ready to accept it. Actress Patricia Tallman feels it is his passion for his cause that initially attracts her character. "He is selfless and he's trying to find what's best for all telepaths," Pat says. "He's talking about something that has been so forbidden for so long, but it feels right, especially for Lyta. She knows firsthand how used, put upon, and then discarded telepaths are, so when he is talking about those issues, she really listens. I think at first, obviously, she thought he was a bag of wind, but she saw he was willing to put his money where his mouth was and she later changed her tune about him."

The two also worked well together and that was important to get the sense of intimacy between them, especially as their relationship became more physical. Robin Atkin Downes has only praise for his fellow actor. "She's an amazing lady all around. She's intelligent, she's smart, she's beautiful, she's talented, and I had a great time working with her. We actually got together and talked about our characters and worked on the scenes, which is, I think, rare in a lot of television work. Usually the first time you work on the scene is when you're rehearsing it right before you shoot it. When we worked together on 'Paragon of Animals,' we got together in her trailer and we talked about the character and we ran through the scene and we just worked on it, and I think it made a big difference when it actually came time to shoot it."

In that scene, Lyta is still somewhat standoffish. She listens to Byron's words, but flinches when he touches her. She has had, as she earlier told Garibaldi, "one hell of a day," being used to scan the mind of a dying man, experiencing his death, and then being approached by Garibaldi to do yet another job without so much as an exchange of pleasantries. She has been hurt many times before and doesn't want to be hurt again. She seems to have buried her emotional core and there is something chilling in the way she tells Byron, "I don't let anybody in anymore." But he is still determined to try. "I think he sees in her a lot of the qualities that Pat has," Robin says. "I don't think she [Lyta] gets the credit she deserves. I also think he senses her power. Byron just welcomes everyone in, and she's somebody who's completely closed herself off. He wants telepaths to open themselves up to that, to embrace and rejoice in this beautiful song that we all have and that we're all connected by."

Byron's description of humanity's history of brutalizing, murdering, and enslaving others for their own purposes has a resonance with the plight of the Enfili. These people are victims of Raiders who have raped their world for what they could take and killed the leaders who might stand in their way. Byron may consider that Human nature has not changed—and with the example of the Psi Corps and mundanes' attitudes to telepaths, maybe he is right—but there is at least an attempt to evolve into something better with the Interstellar Alliance. Sheridan, as president, is the one who moves to shame the Drazi into admitting they are behind the raids and put an end to them, reflecting an evolution in his own nature. "Sheridan has to go from being a soldier to being a diplomat in a more severe fashion because in some ways he had more freedom before," Joe Straczynski explains. "If he had a problem, he would go out and shoot them. He can't do that anymore."

Sheridan's diplomatic moves with the Drazi have two aims. First is to shame the Drazi into admitting to their alliance with the Raiders and bring the raids to an end. Second is to encourage the other ambassadors to sign a Declaration of Principles. The principles were written by G'Kar, who takes to his new task as official scribe to the Interstellar Alliance with great relish. Perhaps one can see something of Joe Straczynski in G'Kar's enthusiasm for his newfound job. But actor Andreas Katsulas doesn't want to draw too much of a comparison between the writing force behind *Babylon 5* and G'Kar. Instead, he puts G'Kar's enthusiasm down to a comment he made at a *Babylon 5* convention. "In response to a question from the floor about where would I like to see G'Kar go in the fifth season, I had mentioned there—and Joe, of course, heard me—that I would like to see some of what G'Kar was writing. The fourth season I was in prison cells writing, I was in my room writing, but we never got to see what I was writing about, and so I think he picked up on that. It's not necessarily that he decided I'd become his spokesperson, but he thought that was a good idea and picked up on it."

The scene reveals a much lighter side to G'Kar than had been seen before. There is a quirky humor to the way G'Kar asks Sheridan to pause while his "muse" is speaking to him and then insists that the ambassadors will have to sign the Declaration all over again because he has thought of a better way to write it! Andreas Katsulas prefers not to refer to it as another side of his character, but rather part of his ongoing development. "He's carried a burden all these years about his people, a sort of paranoia fighting against him, trying to move up against the stream. Now G'Kar is more or less flowing with the stream with this idea that all races are one. He sees things [more clearly], so all of that psychological heaviness is gone now and he moves along in a more positive fashion."

4
"A View from the Gallery"

Cast

President John Sheridan ....Bruce Boxleitner
Michael Garibaldi ....Jerry Doyle
Delenn ....Mira Furlan
Dr. Stephen Franklin ....Richard Biggs
Captain Elizabeth Lochley ....Tracy Scoggins
Zack Allan ....Jeff Conaway
Londo Mollari ....Peter Jurasik
G'Kar ....Andreas Katsulas

Guest Stars

Byron ....Robin Atkin Downes
Lt. David Corwin ....Joshua Cox
Mack ....Raymond O'Connor
Bo ....Lawrence LeJohn

Alien ships stream past a Babylon 5 probe lurking in hyperspace. One fires and the probe is ripped apart, wreckage spinning away in all directions. Back on the station, the alert is sounded. A squadron of armed security forces run to their positions, past two maintenance men who are working at an inspection panel in the corridor. One of them, Mack, climbs down from his inspection stall and stands at least a foot shorter than his colleague, Bo. "Seems like every week something goes wrong around here," Bo reflects. "And we have to clean it up," his friend responds.

Bo is called to Medlab where Dr. Franklin wants him to take a look at the isolab. He needs it to be ready to treat aliens wounded from the fight that is coming. Bo wonders why anyone would want to help people who are coming to kill them, and Franklin answers by telling him about the time his father was captured by enemy

forces. After two months, EarthForce eventually
liberated the enemy base, and the young Stephen
Franklin watched his father and two other injured
soldiers being brought out alive on ISN. "The base
doctor had kept them alive over the objections of the
CO because he believed that life was sacred and had to
be preserved," he says. "When I saw him walk out,
supported by the doctor, I knew right then that that's
what I wanted to do with my life."

Mack, meanwhile, has been asked to fix the secondary
targeting console in C&C. He crawls underneath the
desk just as the first wave of alien ships bursts through
the jumpgate. Starfuries swarm to intercept, the defense
grid primaries fire, and two ships are destroyed. A third
tries to make a run for it. "I want that ship" orders
Captain Lochley as it heads toward the jumpgate, but
the only guns that can reach it are the secondaries,
which are still off-line. Mack pulls a large alien insect
out of the wiring and the targeting console bursts back
into life. The secondary guns fire and hit the third ship
just seconds from the jumpgate. One of its wings is
blown away and the whole thing explodes.

A second wave of alien ships swarms in, and while the
fighting continues outside, a breaching pod attaches
itself to the station's hull, spilling alien soldiers onto
Babylon 5. Bo and Mack are taking a transport tube to
one of the shelters when the power fails and they land
up right in the middle of a fight. Zack shouts at them to
get out of the way, and they sink to their bellies,
crawling off while gunfire and hand-to-hand combat
continue above them.

After an eerie encounter with Byron and the telepaths,
during which Bo learns what it feels like to pilot a
Starfury, the maintenance men are eventually able to rest
near a portal where they have a view of what is going on
outside. "The cavalry's here!" cries Mack as a flurry of
jump points appear and a fleet of White Stars spills out,
firing at the alien ships.

When the fighting stops, Bo and Mack walk through

the shelters on their way back to work. "Typical," Mack
says, looking around at all the rubbish strewn around
the place. "They call all the shots, get all the glory, and
leave it to us to clean up all the time!" Then they turn
the corner into the customs area and see more than a
dozen bodies laid out on the floor. Dr. Franklin is
moving from one person to another, checking them, then
throwing a sheet over their dead faces. "Well . . . maybe
not all the mess," Bo reflects.

The script for "A View from the Gallery" was written in one overnight session by Joe Straczynski, who faced an incredible workload at the beginning of the fifth season. With all the delays incurred through negotiations to secure *Babylon 5*'s new home on TNT, he was left with a daunting schedule. Confirmation that the season was going ahead came one month later than usual, which meant he had to get cracking on coming up with a bunch of scripts so the production could get to work. "I ended up writing four or five scripts in about four weeks, during which time I also went to three conventions. I was spending time writing in the back of cars going to and from airports, on trains coming from Blackpool to London, on planes, in hotel rooms, and trying to pull it all together," Joe recalls. [*TV Zone*, issue 99] "'A View from the Gallery' all came out of my keyboard in one day between 4 P.M. and 3 A.M."

Unusually for a *Babylon 5* script, it went through several further revisions during production, including the introduction of the Medlab scene and the whole scene with Byron and the telepaths when Bo experienced what it would be like to be a Starfury pilot. The revisions became necessary when the episode began coming in short, due to the guest stars having rehearsed so well and so much that their scenes were done in record time.

The idea for the episode originally came from *Babylon 5*'s creative consultant Harlan Ellison and worked in a similar way to Season Two's "And Now for a Word." The two maintenance men, Bo and Mack, watch the events on the station from a distance and allow the audience to step back a little bit, too. Rather than being involved in the action at the top level, the audience is an observer, seeing Sheridan and Delenn's relationship and watching Lochley deal with the situation as an outsider might. "One of the things I always do is look for ways to turn the series format on its head and show us our characters from other perspectives, since perspective is so much at the heart of the show," Joe Straczynski says. "Whether that's jumping forward in time or an ISN documentary or seeing everything through the eyes of a third party—or two—it's always a risk because it's never what one expects to see, and a lot of people like to see what they expect to see."

It also relies a lot on the performances of the two guest stars, in this case Raymond O'Connor as Mack and Lawrence LeJohn as Bo. "The casting was very important," director Janet Greek acknowledges. "A lot of really talented people came in and read for that, and we went for two people who were actors first and comedians second. Some really quite famous comics came in and read for them, but Joe and I both wanted them to be people who were really grounded in reality, and so we went for those two guys and I think they worked really well. And they were a riot—both of them are really talented—and especially Ray, the shorter one, was quite a comedian and really had a great dry sense of humor. It was just a lot of fun working with them."

Their contrasting physical types also make them a fun pairing. The fact that one was black and the other white was specified in the script, but having a tall one and a short one was not and helped make them quite a comic duo. "I loved that, too—they just looked funny together," Janet says. "I liked the opening scene where I put Ray up on a box so he looks pretty much the same size [as Lawrence]. When you first meet them they're working on a console that is behind all of these troops that are going through, so when the troops left, I pushed in on them. They were talking, and then, all of a sudden, Ray steps down off this box and you realize he is very short compared to Lawrence, who's very tall. That amused me a lot. I did a lot of things like that in the show that personally amused me."

Another advantage of taking an outsider's view is that one can question things that usually go unquestioned. Franklin's attitude to treating the enemy wounded is one such question. Bo's attitude that he would not lift a finger to save someone who had come to kill him is understandable. But who could disagree with Franklin's philosophy that all life is sacred after Richard Biggs delivered such a passionate speech? "The scene was written on a Friday and I was to deliver it on a Monday morning," Rick remembers. "It was such an emotional, personal scene, I really wanted to work as much as I could on it and deliver as much truth to it as possible. It really says a lot about the character and what he feels and what he would do. Dr. Franklin has said many times that he would die for patients, he would die to keep secrets about patients, so it says a lot about the character and how passionate he is and how serious he is in what he does."

When Bo and Mack are back together and in a shelter away from the fighting, they eavesdrop on an exchange between Londo and G'Kar. There is much more of a relaxed feeling between these two former enemies now, and after several minutes of their bickering, Mack turns to Bo with the remark, "How long you figure they've been married?"

"Isn't that great?" Peter Jurasik, who plays Londo, says with a chuckle. "Joe's been trying to squeeze out as many different facets of this relationship as he can, so this is just one more wonderful facet. You certainly can see them that way. Andreas, I'm sure, will certainly cop to the fact that after five years there is an aspect of . . . We arrive on the set in the morning, and it's 'who are we doing scenes with? It's not he and I again? Oh my God!' There is an aspect of the married couple in it, I suppose. It's a wonderful relationship, G'kar and Londo."

Their exchange as they sit in the shelter with nothing much else to do is unexpectedly revealing. It reminds G'Kar of his childhood being bombed by the Centauri, and despite the horrific circumstances, there is a fondness in the way G'Kar remembers the singing, the praying, the eating and sleeping that the Narn did to keep their spirits up. Londo's childhood was very different. Compared to G'Kar he lived a life of luxury, but there is only sadness in Londo as he remembers his younger days in which responsibility was always thrust upon him.

"That's the brilliant thing that we should all be grateful to Joe about," Andreas Katsulas, who plays G'Kar, says. "He's had more time to concentrate on little revelations about all the characters. In the fourth season he had to get the story out, he had to crank it out, we thought it was the end. This year it sort of settled back, he really fleshed out these characters and I think it's great, I'm very happy with how the fifth season worked out."

"It certainly does say something about who Londo is and why he's made up the way he is and how he reacts to things," Peter adds. "But it also speaks to Centauri society, it speaks about growing up on a royal level. My brother-in-law, his father was a royal painter for the Indian government. He painted for that family and some of his paintings are in the British Museum—he's quite famous actually—but he grew up in that environment. I got to chat a little bit with him, and it really is a world unto itself and the children are involved in that. It speaks to that in the Centauri world, too, that it's a very rarefied air to grow up in the royal court like Londo did.

"When G'Kar talks about his childhood in that same scene, I think what I was playing in Londo is that he can't even believe that this is true. It's like someone making up something, like someone saying to him 'Aliens landed in my backyard last night and we took a Jacuzzi together and then we went inside and had an omelette and breakfast and read the paper.' You think, what are you talking about?! That's the way Londo is because he comes from this rarefied world. His reaction to G'Kar is, 'I can't even imagine what you're talking about. You mean you didn't have responsibilities?' "

The episode is full of little character moments like this, but ultimately it is about the way the ordinary man sees the events that are shaping his life around him. While an alien fleet is on its way to destroy the station, Bo and Mack are talking about sandwiches, of all things. All hell may be breaking loose outside, but they just keep doing their jobs without really being able to see the big picture. They talk about sandwiches, because how can they relate to the space battle? Just every once in a while they get a glimpse of what the people in the front line are living with and realize, as Bo says in the episode, "it's bigger than anyone should ever have to deal with."

5
"Learning Curve"

Cast

President John Sheridan	Bruce Boxleitner
Michael Garibaldi	Jerry Doyle
Delenn	Mira Furlan
Dr. Stephen Franklin	Richard Biggs
Captain Elizabeth Lochley	Tracy Scoggins
Zack Allan	Jeff Conaway

Guest Stars

Rastenn	Nathan Anderson
Turval	Turhan Bey
Tannier	Brendan Ford
Trace	Trevor Goddard
Durhan	Brian McDermott
Enforcer	Mongo Brownlee
Security Guard	Dawn Comer
Teegarden	Erica Ortega

Durhan, an experienced Minbari warrior and Ranger, interrupts a group of recruits in meditation to ask their teacher, Turval, if he will accompany him to Babylon 5. Turval chooses two of his most restless students, Tannier and Rastenn, to be his escorts. "Babylon 5," Tannier says with awe, "the home of peace."

In Babylon 5's Down Below sector, a man is thrown against a wall with such force that he collapses to the ground. A PPG is aimed at him, and in a flash of plasma he is shot dead. "Leave the body where they'll see it," says the man's assailant, Trace. "Make sure they understand that there's a new power in town."

Zack looks over the body that has been dumped in Down Below, watched by a crowd keeping an uncertain distance. "I don't suppose any of you saw anything?" he asks. Trace is watching all of this closely and senses Zack is a clever man who might just persuade someone

to inform on him. He tells his henchmen that Zack must
be killed. Tonight.

A woman called Teegarden nervously approaches
Trace and his group of thugs. She sent a message to
Zack to meet her in Down Below, just as they had
requested, and now she wants her payment. She takes
the credit chit Trace hands her, but stops when she
overhears their plans for Zack. "You didn't say anything
about killing anyone," she protests, backing away
toward the door. "I can't go along with this."

Tannier and Rastenn hear Teegarden's screams
echoing down the corridor, and Tannier runs to her aid.
He turns the corner to see her being dragged before
Trace, who pulls out a PPG and aims it at her. At that
moment Tannier extends his fighting pike. Trace turns at
the noise and fires. Tannier leaps out of the way and
knocks the woman's captor to the ground. He throws his
pike like a javelin, knocking the gun from Trace's hand,
allowing the woman to run to safety. But he does not see
the man behind him who strikes him across the head
with a metal bar. Trace looks down at the barely
conscious Minbari and decides that the death of this
rookie Ranger, instead of Zack, will make a good
enough statement to the authorities. Trace kicks Tannier
hard in the stomach and the others join in, punching and
kicking in a brutal scrum.

Durhan looks at Tannier lying injured in Medlab and
turns to Delenn. "Mora'dum," he says. The word refers
to a part of Ranger training, Delenn explains to Dr.
Franklin. It means, "the application of terror."

When Tannier is well enough to stand, but not fully
healed, the others take him back to Down Below where
he confronts Trace. Tannier stands ready with his pike
extended and throws down a second pike for Trace, but
Trace refuses to fight. So Tannier strikes a smarting blow
across Trace's head, and Trace picks up the pike. The
thug retaliates, but his every blow is deflected by his
Minbari opponent. Tannier follows up with a rally of
strikes, each one hitting home until Trace is knocked to

the ground. Trace staggers to his feet and throws the pike down in disgust. Tannier also lets his pike drop and moves in with his fists, hitting Trace in the stomach, the face, and the stomach again until he collapses unconscious to the floor.

Tannier announces to Durhan that his fear is now gone. He feels only pity for this man whose name will be forgotten. His own name, Tannier says, doesn't belong to history or the world, but "it belongs to me." Durhan smiles. The lesson is ended.

"That was an interesting one," director David Eagle says, recalling his work on "Learning Curve." "Because it was the first time for me on the show where the majority of work was done with guest stars, guest actors, as opposed to the majority being done by the regular cast. It's sometimes tougher because what's great about the regular cast is they know their characters for the most part, they know the style of the show, they know me because we've worked together. So it tends to be less difficult to work with the regular cast, we all kind of know what to expect from one another. You have four new characters in "Learning Curve," all of whom are Minbari, none of whom know anything about the Minbari or much about *Babylon 5* or the regular characters or their own characters. So for me, as a director, it means a lot more work, it means a lot more preparation, it means spending a lot more time with those actors talking about what their character is about and how their character would deal with that particular situation that they're faced with.

"With the regular characters I can usually rely on them knowing right off the bat how their character will react to something and I just need to go in there and make a few adjustments. Here, you've got actors who are doing this for the first time and are not that familiar with the show. It's starting out fresh, it's like starting out with a fresh canvas and fresh paint and painting a new picture, as opposed to working with the regulars where the canvas already has a lot of paint on it and a lot of people have contributed. So, on the one hand it's a lot more work, on the other hand it also can be a lot of fun and very rewarding from a directorial standpoint."

The only familiar face in *Babylon 5* terms to feature in the list of guest actors for this episode is Turhan Bey, who previously played the Centauri emperor in Season Two's "The Coming of Shadows." Back then, everybody on the show was said to be sad that his character was killed off so quickly because they had found him charming to work with. Did Mira Furlan have the same impression when she worked alongside him in this episode? "He's wonderful and lovely and I enjoyed when he came in," Mira, who plays Delenn, laughs. "He's this incredibly gentle and sweet and fine human being, from another world. He actually reminded me of the world where I'm coming from, which is central Europe. I mean Austria, he's from Austria, we spoke German when he came, and German is the language of my childhood because my grandmother spoke German to me when I was a kid. He reminded me of that whole world and the level of education that is not there anymore. It's getting lost. It was just normal to speak a couple of languages and it was normal to communicate with all those different cultures that are mixing, that are like a little melting pot. That whole Austro-Hungarian empire was definitely a reality for me when I was growing up, though we lived in a communist or socialist Yugoslavia. My grandmother came from that world, and she studied in Graz and she studied in Paris and she traveled all around Europe and spoke German and French, so he was definitely coming from that world and had that finesse. I loved him."

"Learning Curve," by concentrating on a set of characters that haven't been seen on the show before and won't be seen again—at least as far as the fifth season is concerned—is not the standard way of doing a *Babylon 5* episode. But then, what is? One of the things *Babylon 5* has always been is different, and not only different from other shows, but different from itself. There is always a surprise around the corner, whether it be an episode that consists entirely of an ISN report, as with Season Two's "And Now for a Word," or an episode of two people, one the prisoner, the other the interrogator, locked in a battle of wills, as with Season Four's "Intersections in Real Time." Season Five takes more departures from the norm. This is only the fifth episode of the season and already the audience has been treated to an episode inside Londo's head and another from the point of view of two maintenance men. "Learning Curve" is another example of J. Michael Straczynski's different approach to the fifth year. "In the first eleven or twelve episodes, almost half the shows are off format in one way or another," he says. "I enjoy those things because they are muscles you have as a writer that you don't exercise all the time . . . One of the things I wanted to do was try new things. It's the fifth year, I can experiment. They can't do anything to me if I do experiment, they can't throw me into jail, they can't cancel my show. So I thought I would take the opportunity, instead of being comfortable during the fifth season doing same old . . . , same old . . . , same old . . . , to experiment, to try different formats, different approaches to it, go off format. What's the worst that will happen? That an episode won't work—that's about it." [*Dreamwatch,* issue 45]

It is a chance to explore the Rangers or, in the Minbari language, the "Anla'shok." Back in Season Three's "A Late Delivery from Avalon," Marcus told Franklin something of his training: that he was taught how to live, to breathe, to fight, to die, and that he was taught terror, how to use it and how to face it. When Franklin says he would like to hear more, Marcus becomes distant; "No, you wouldn't," he says, and turns away. That moment sets up a question of what horrors Marcus had to endure in Ranger training, and it is answered two years later when Tannier experiences the mora'dum, a lesson in terror.

Tannier is taught how to face his own terror and how to use it when, still recovering from his injuries, he is brought back to face the man responsible for beating him almost to death. It is also a lesson for Trace, the thug from Down Below, who is made to face his own nature. As Turval tells the other Ranger students who are gathered around, he is an archetype bully who is essentially a coward and who gets others to do his dirty work for him. Now that the others are eliminated, he has to fight his own fight and suffer the consequences of the violence he meted out to Tannier. The coward is no match for the Minbari, even in his weakened state, and Tannier triumphs over his own terror and, in the process, learns about himself. In saying his name belongs to him and not history or the world, the lesson also speaks to his fellow Ranger trainee, Rastenn. Earlier in the episode Rastenn seemed to hanker after glory, preferring the challenge of "standing alone, unarmed, prepared to die" to the challenge of meditation. It is more important, the episode suggests, to know yourself before you have to stand alone—a reflection of the philosophy learned from the Vorlons and the Shadows that you should first answer the question "Who are you?" before you ask "What do you want?"

But the episode does not entirely concentrate on the outside characters; there are other threads building through this episode, mostly concerning Lochley. Garibaldi is determined to find out which side she fought on during the Earth civil war, suspecting—quite rightly—that she was on the other side. She responds by giving such a speech about the ethics of being a soldier that it elicits a round of applause from the mess hall. "I think the bottom line is she really believed she was doing the right thing," actress Tracy Scoggins says. "I think that's one of the definitions of integrity. It's funny, it reminds me of a quote from, I think it was Winston Churchill. He said 'We hope our principal men are men of principles,' and I think that's where she stands."

"Tracy, I have to tell you, has been wonderful," director David Eagle adds. "'Learning Curve' was my first time working with her and she had a huge scene with Jerry Doyle [Garibaldi], I think it was four and a half pages long and it was mostly her talking—that's a lot to throw on somebody, and if you're not prepared to do a long scene like that then everybody's in trouble. But she even called me a day or two before to ask me some questions about the scene, and then she came in just knowing it inside out and really made it happen. I really appreciated that and found she was a joy to work with."

The episode ends with an uncomfortable moment between Sheridan and Delenn. Even before the scene began, he told her something that was clearly uncomfortable for her to hear. Whatever it was, it involves Lochley, and that raises a question about their relationship that teases viewers into the next episode.

6

"Strange Relations"

Cast

President John Sheridan	Bruce Boxleitner
Michael Garibaldi	Jerry Doyle
Delenn	Mira Furlan
Dr. Stephen Franklin	Richard Biggs
Captain Elizabeth Lochley	Tracy Scoggins
Zack Allan	Jeff Conaway
Lyta Alexander	Patricia Tallman
Londo Mollari	Peter Jurasik
G'Kar	Andreas Katsulas

Guest Stars

Byron	Robin Atkin Downes
Lt. David Corwin	Joshua Cox
Bester	Walter Koenig
Security Guard	Clynell Jackson III
Bloodhound Teep #1	James Lew
Telepath	Clarke Coleman
Bloodhound Teep #2	Steven Hal Lambert

Lyta carries a bundle of medical supplies to Down Below where Byron's rogue telepaths have made a roughshod home. She tries to persuade him to take some of the vitamins and get more rest, but as they talk, he turns his head to one side, suddenly distracted. The other telepaths sense it, too—Bester and a troop of Psi Corps bloodhound units have come to hunt them down.

Garibaldi storms into Lochley's office where she is sipping tea with Bester. "You son of a—" Garibaldi launches forward and Lochley stands to block him. She orders him back, but Garibaldi is enraged at the memory of what Bester did to his mind. "You don't understand!" he yells, and steps forward again, but this time Lochley pulls back her fist and strikes him in the jaw. He is startled for a moment and, in that moment, Lochley orders security to escort him to the brig.

Bester takes his bloodhounds to Down Below where he finds Lyta standing alone. There is a telepathic silence all around them, a sign that Lyta is blocking every stray thought that might betray the whereabouts of the rogues. Bester orders one of the men to check the hall, but as he moves forward a telepathic slap whips him around the face. Another man moves and feels Lyta's mind slap him, harder this time. Bester himself is forced to retreat, but he'll be back. Lyta urges Byron to scatter his people across the station, and he thanks her, kissing her gently on the lips.

Lochley enters the cell where Garibaldi is being held, determined to have it out with him. He's been rummaging through her personal files because he has a feeling there is more to her appointment than Sheridan simply wanting to make a statement by hiring someone from the other side during the war. Lochley tells him the other reason comes down to trust, and Sheridan knows he can trust her because they were once married. "Get outta town!" Garibaldi says, starting to chuckle. "If I worked at it for a hundred years, I never could've come up with that one."

Londo, Delenn decides, needs a bodyguard. A sabotage attempt recently destroyed a cruiser he was due to take back to Centauri Prime, demonstrating how much danger he is in. And while Londo's enemies have a clear shot at him, the Alliance is in danger of losing one of its most important allies. Delenn suggests G'Kar for the job. "Just think what a symbol it would make to have a Narn guarding the life of a Centauri," she says. G'Kar is taken aback, but soon the idea starts to appeal.

Bester's Hounds have all but rounded up the rogue telepaths and Byron has decided to give himself up. Lyta protests, but Byron is adamant. "My people need me and I must go to them," he says. "Good-bye, Lyta."

Lochley is in a dilemma with the telepath situation. The president has told her Bester can't take them, yet the

*Psi Cop has Earth law on his side. It is only when
Franklin tells her that Delenn and G'Kar have asked him
to research interspecies diseases on behalf of the Alliance
that the solution comes to her. She gets Franklin to put it
in writing, then slaps it in front of Bester. The telepaths
have been wandering all over the galaxy picking up
who-knows-what diseases and, as such, they are subject
to a sixty-day quarantine. Bester is forced to concede.
"I'll wait the sixty days," he tells Lochley. "Just keep an
eye on them, Captain . . . because sooner or later, they
will turn on you."*

The mystery of why Sheridan appointed Lochley to run Babylon 5 is finally resolved with Lochley's confession to Garibaldi that they were once married. The admission of her mistake, of briefly falling in love with a fellow soldier and getting married in the heat of the moment, only to fall out of love again, opens her character out a little bit. We see a little more of her humanity and of the frailty that lies behind her tough exterior. "I have a theory about this," actress Tracy Scoggins says. "I think when Lochley first arrived here at a new command—I think you can't show people your weaknesses too much. In the beginning, if she seemed very all-business, that is crucial to maintaining the power that you need to have when you step into a new command post, especially when your loyalty is doubted by so many. I loved the way Joe gradually, over the season, has exposed her soft underbelly a little bit here and there and shown her flaws. My dad had a great saying that I used to love—he had a lot of them—but my dad used to say 'Show them your strength and they'll take notice, show them your weakness and they'll take heart.' I really think that's true. I really think you need to show them the strength in the beginning. It's funny, I looked on the Internet and saw what people speculated and not many people guessed that we were married. I love the way Joe shocks people sometimes."

One of those who was surprised by this revelation was Bruce Boxleitner. The show had built Sheridan up to be a man who was devoted to the women he fell in love with—

first Anna, whose death he had to come to terms with before allowing himself to fall in love again, and then Delenn.

The disclosure could have served to put a rift between Sheridan and Delenn, but she accepts her husband's decision because it is right for the sake of the station. "Delenn is above our little human flaws and jealousies, so she's wise, we know that," Mira Furlan, who plays Delenn, says.

"This season was kind of strange for me and I had a lot of questions for myself," she continues. "Somehow, my character went for the big picture, the political picture. I, personally, think that politics is a disgusting thing and I just have this organic refusal to accept politicians as human beings. Which is my problem. I don't say that's the right attitude, and there's probably good politicians and bad politicians, but I'm just one of those people who can't share that view—there is something very antiauthoritarian in me."

The main plot of the episode, however, deals with the telepaths. By allowing them to live on Babylon 5, Sheridan created a dilemma for the station, which is under Earth jurisdiction. By Earth law, all rogue telepaths have to be handed over to the Psi Corps. This opens the way for a return appearance by Walter Koenig's Bester, which always adds a sinister undertone to an episode. There are always issues that surface when Bester is around; this time that means Garibaldi. Garibaldi has not had a chance to settle the score since Bester programmed him to sell out Sheridan, nearly getting both of them killed in the fourth season. Understandably, Garibaldi approaches Bester in a rage, and Lochley only stops him by slugging him in the face.

These sorts of scenes are not the easiest to choreograph because the actors have to make it look real without putting each other in the hospital. "If it happens, it happens," actor Jerry Doyle says with a typically gung-ho attitude. "The only thing you want the other actor or the stunt person to do is, if they hit you, don't stop. Don't go 'Oh shit, I don't believe I hit him!' because if you make contact you might as well finish the scene because you're not going to get much more real than that. If there's blood shooting out of your eye, people go 'Wow, that looks real!' and that's because it is! Besides, as soon as you yell 'cut,' you've got to back it up and do it all over again. But she [Tracy] was good, she walked in and threw a right. The way I came up, I was pissed at Bester, but I tried to play Garibaldi's attitude like 'okay, nice shot.' I was more impressed with her than really pissed off, and she really gave me a wake-up call: if it's not going to happen now, then it's not going to happen."

With Garibaldi in the brig, Bester is free to chase the telepaths and renew his acquaintance with Lyta, the telepath he forced back into the Psi Corps after the Shadow War. Rejoining was something she did reluctantly and it left unfinished business between the two of them. This time when they meet, it is Lyta who has the advantage, using her powers to lash out at Bester's men. "I think she finally stepped up to the plate on that one," actress Patricia Tallman says. "She'd been dancing around Bester a little bit—partly, I believe, because she doesn't really know what she can do. But now she has a reason to stand up to him for the other telepaths."

However, she is not strong enough to protect them all, and one by one they are rounded up. Lyta sees them in custody and looks to Zack, but not even the man who tried to befriend her the previous year will look her in the eye now. She turns away in despair, not knowing what to do. "There's a whole lot in the first half of the season for Lyta where I kept going back to Joe [Straczynski] and going 'Now come on, she's got to do something' and he's like 'nope, nope, she doesn't do anything.' 'What do you mean she doesn't do anything?' We would be having these discussions and it was so frustrating, he wouldn't really tell me why. I had never really challenged Joe like that before, I'd always taken what he had given me and gone 'Okay, whatever you say,' but this time I was really insistent. I'm going, 'I don't know how she's supposed to watch all this stuff go on and she's got these powers, but she doesn't do anything with them?' And he says, 'No, she doesn't, but this is going to catapult her into something else,' and that was vague enough to drive me crazy!"

A smaller thread of the episode involves an assassination attempt on Londo and the realization that he is in danger.

When the cruiser that was supposed to be taking him home explodes, Lochley ventures outside in a Starfury to inspect the damage and on her helmet we see a phoenix insignia. It is only a small detail, but one that Tracy Scoggins was stunned by. "My whole life I've been fairly obsessed with the legend of the phoenix," she says. "I would draw them, I would embroider them on my jeans. Then I'm handed a script and I'm reading and 'Lochley's Starfury helmet's insignia is a phoenix.' I called Joe immediately and said, 'Okay, you've been talking to my mom, you've been talking to my girl-friends back home in Texas?' And he said, 'No, no.' I said, 'What's the deal here? How did you come to pick that for Lochley?' He goes, 'It just seemed appropriate.' "

The resolution of the assassination attempt on Londo is to assign G'Kar as his bodyguard. Considering these two proud statesmen were once at war, it is a highly ironic move, and one that continues to push these two characters together as events unfold in the rest of the season.

7

"Secrets of the Soul"

Cast

Dr. Stephen Franklin ....Richard Biggs
Zack Allan ....Jeff Conaway
Lyta Alexander ....Patricia Tallman

Guest Stars

Byron ....Robin Atkin Downes
Kirrin ....Fiona Dwyer
Peter ....Jack Hannibal
Carl ....Stuart McLean
Ambassador Tal ....Jana Robbins
Thug ....Roger Hewlett
Security Guard ....Skip Stellrecht
Drazi Captain ....William Scudder

Dr. Franklin explains to the Hyach ambassador, Tal, that he will need their medical records if he is to research the dangers posed to both them and others through cross-species infection. Tal agrees, but after Franklin leaves, Tal's attaché questions the decision. "This is a mistake," he says. "What if he finds out?"

Peter, a telekinetic come to seek refuge with Byron's people, is stopped in a darkened hallway by a bunch of thugs. Carl, the leader, calls him a freak and shoves him back against the wall. Peter looks at an old piece of pipe lying discarded against the opposite wall and it shakes in the grip of his thoughts, flies across the room, and hits Carl in the stomach. Angered, Carl leads the others forward, and Peter is powerless to stop their feet and fists hitting him over and over again.

An avenging group of telepaths advances on one of Carl's men, planting an illusion in his mind. He screams, seeing his arms and legs on fire. When Byron gets there, he stops them. But as he kneels to calm the

man down, Zack brings a security team around the
corner and Byron is arrested.

Byron paces around the cell, fearing what his people
will do without him. An image flashes into his mind of
Carl being hit in the stomach, then across the face, and
then struck over the head with a pipe. Byron looks
helplessly at the bars of the cell, sensing the man being
beaten to death.

Franklin is wrestling with the medical and genetic
records given to him by the Hyach. Despite a civilization
going back seven millennia, they only have medical
records going back eight hundred years. He eventually
finds an old Drazi record mentioning a species called the
"Hyach-doh," which gives him a clue to what they are
hiding.

Ambassador Tal admits the Hyach-doh were another
sentient species on their planet that were deliberately
wiped out. It was a shameful genocide that came at a
price. Only now have they discovered that their race
depended on interbreeding with the Hyach-doh. With
them gone, their birthrate is falling and they will
eventually die out. Franklin offers to help them, but only
if their secret is revealed to the Alliance to enable a
pooling of resources to find a solution. The Hyach elders
have ordered that the matter be kept secret, but Tal
agrees nevertheless. "The price is too high otherwise,"
he says.

Byron is released from the brig, but is disconsolate,
knowing that his own people have killed Carl. "I should
have taught them better," he tells Lyta. She tries to
comfort him, removing her jacket and unbuttoning his
shirt. She sits, half naked, in front and before they get
closer she warns that he may be burned by the changes
the Vorlons made in her. "Then let it burn," Byron says.

Telepathic walls are broken down as Byron and Lyta
make love. He sees her memories of carrying a Vorlon
inside of her and of fighting the Shadows. Her eyes turn
black, but they continue to make love, their minds and
their bodies intertwined. As they go deeper, Byron senses

Lyta floating in a clear tube of liquid while around her float alien fetuses and adult beings in row upon row of tubes.

The images give Byron a new sense of purpose. Knowing the Vorlons created telepaths to save normals in the Shadow War gives him a lever with which to bargain with the mundanes. He turns to his followers. "They owe us a place where we can be among our own kind," he tells them.

"Secrets of the Soul" examines Byron's beliefs and dreams for his people. He arrived on Babylon 5 hoping to find a better life for his followers, but only found a temporary resting place. His telepaths are still treated with suspicion, and sometimes scorn, by the normals who make up the majority and fear them because they are different.

His attitude has won over a once-suspicious Lyta, who can be seen alongside Byron at almost every turn in this episode, having once again turned her back on the Psi Corps. In an impassioned speech to Zack she explains why she believes in Byron and why he is the one to have turned her life around. Zack responds with the suspicion felt by many of those on the station and with a hint of jealousy. "Yeah, well, he is jealous," Jeff Conaway, who plays Zack, says. "He really has some pretty deep feelings for Lyta. I think he identifies with her in many ways, kind of being on the outside a little bit and kind of having no home. Babylon 5 is his home now, but he's really just getting used to it, he's trusting it. He didn't trust anything for a long time because of his past life and his behavior, and so he's feeling a lot more solid. With Lyta I'm basically saying, 'Come on, how about it?' We're sharing pizzas together, then the next thing you know, some creep shows up that can do things with his mind and she's off and running—the tramp!" Jeff chuckles to himself, not meaning the comment seriously. "I now call her the devil mistress of the universe."

Byron's overriding principle is that telepaths are different from mundanes, that they shouldn't resort to violence to solve problems. It is a noble and difficult course to follow, but it has a certain power, as Byron proves when he stands up to a group of thugs in Down Below. He invites the leader to hit him, which he does again and again. But when Byron simply stands there and takes it, his attacker finds violence is no fun anymore. "The punches missed me probably by about three inches," Robin Atkin Downes, who plays Byron, says. "Basically, we ran through the scene and when it came down to the punches—this is before they started shooting it—we did it in slow motion. Then you do it in half time, and then you do it at full speed. Then we shot it from all different sides and we did it about fifty times, and so after throwing my head back for so many times it was sore for about the next three weeks. But it was fun. I think that scene turned out really well and the writing was great."

Nevertheless, not everyone can live by such an idealistic principle, and Byron knows deep within himself that if he is not with his people, they will resort to violence to protect themselves. Perhaps this is the secret of his soul, that he knows that his belief in a superior telepathic race that doesn't resort to violence is more a dream than a reality. Without him, they used their powers to punish one of the men that beat up the young telekinetic, Peter. Then, later, they physically beat the leader of the thugs to death. Byron blames himself for not teaching them better, but in reality the fault lies in human nature.

Lyta tries to comfort him by, for the first time since she had been changed by the Vorlons, making love. Never before had *Babylon 5* shown two characters being so intimate, and it is somewhat uncharacteristic for the show. "What I was trying to do was make it very beautiful," director Tony Dow says. "And I wanted it to be very tasteful.

"We talked quite a bit about it," he continues. "I know that [producers] Joe and John were a little concerned because when I talked to Pat about doing it, we were talking about different kinds of body suits and things that she could wear. I said, 'Obviously the best thing would be if you don't wear anything, so then we're not limited by having to hide anything or shoot around things.' She actually agreed, that was what she wanted to do. But as we got closer she was a little bit more nervous about things, so we were very careful to clear the set and there was nobody there who didn't need to be there and it was handled in a real sensitive kind of way."

"It was horrifying, totally horrifying," Pat Tallman says, remembering her first time virtually naked in a TV studio. "Why did they wait until I'm this age and I've had a baby already? Why only now do I get to take my clothes off?! It was a catch-22 because if I had to get naked in front of a crew at least it was these guys that I've worked with for five years and they're totally awesome and I trust them and I love them and we're all good friends, but at the same time that made it hard. But they couldn't have been more lovely, more supportive."

"I've never shot a love scene before on camera," Robin adds. "It was very bizarre. They had a closed set so it was just the director and the DP and I think they had one of the lighting guys. It felt very removed at some point. We wanted to make it realistic, but it was very awkward, in that it was all done with a handheld camera and I was constantly having to block things that weren't supposed to find their way into the view of the camera. It was very technical at times and a little awkward. When we were kissing and stuff that was nice, but the whole rocking back and forth was strange."

When Lyta had first met Byron in "The Paragon of Animals" she had told him that she doesn't let anyone into her mind anymore. Now—echoing Talia Winters' comments to Sinclair about telepaths making love in "Mind War"—Lyta removes that final barrier and Byron enters her mind. What he finds there are images that she has never revealed to anyone else, images of being altered by the Vorlons and of alien babies in artificial wombs, growing into adult telepaths. "Weren't they amazing?" Tony Dow says. "There was a lot of discussion about the tanks. The first thing they suggested was they'll be dry and we'll put some bubbles in front of them or we'll shoot through some water or whatever. But that was actually one of the things I was adamant about, I really wanted to put her in water and have everything in the tanks, and I think it pays off, it really looks very real."

"I actually got in a big tube of water," Pat remembers. "There was this regulator hookup—they called it the hookah—that was in the bottom of the tank so I could breathe on it while I was hanging out in there. When it was time to go, I put it down, we waited for the bubbles to disperse, and then we'd shoot. Earlier, I'd had the two scenes in Byron's quarters, one where I'm cleaning up his wound and the other scene just before the sex scene, and the sex scene, and the underwater scene—all in one day! The underwater part was the easiest part of my day. I got in that tube and just hung out."

Lyta, in this moment, finally reveals the secrets of her soul, while in the other main plot thread of the episode, Franklin is trying to uncover another secret, that of the Hyach. "I think it was a wonderful mystery," actor Richard Biggs says. "Again in that episode, he refers to not giving up their [genetic and medical] information, the very seriousness of patient/doctor confidentiality, and that 'Yes, I would put my life on the line to keep the information that you give me private.' "

The horrific extermination of the Hyach-doh by the Hyach relates to events much closer to home. Although Franklin specifically mentions the Neanderthals—an ancient, extinct humanlike race now believed to have evolved separately from Homo sapiens—it brings to mind more Nazi Germany's genocide of the Jewish people and the more recent "ethnic cleansing" of the former Yugoslavia and Rwanda. "I never really looked at it from a racial point of view," Rick says. "I looked at it more as we don't realize what other races and what other types of people can bring to our own existence and how important different people are to making our lives more interesting and alive."

And perhaps that is the ultimate underlying message of this episode, that by alienating rather than embracing telepaths, the Human race is setting itself up for problems further down the road.

8

"In the Kingdom of the Blind"

Cast

President John Sheridan	Bruce Boxleitner
Michael Garibaldi	Jerry Doyle
Delenn	Mira Furlan
Zack Allan	Jeff Conaway
Lyta Alexander	Patricia Tallman
Londo Mollari	Peter Jurasik
G'Kar	Andreas Katsulas

Guest Stars

Byron	Robin Atkin Downes
Minister Vitari	Neil Hunt
Regent	Damian London
Telepath	Victor Love
Minister Vole	Francis X. McCarthy
Lord Jano	Ian Ogilvy
Drazi	David Darling

Garibaldi hands Sheridan a report showing an increasing number of attacks on shipping lanes. It looks like typical Raider activity, except that in each case the cargoes are destroyed along with any witnesses or evidence. Sheridan paces his office. If they don't find out who's responsible, he considers, they're going to have a real problem on their hands.

"I see you've brought your own entertainment with you," Minister Vitari declares, regarding G'Kar, as Londo brings him into the Centauri royal palace. Londo looks the minister straight in the eye and tells him that G'Kar is his bodyguard. Vitari raises an eyebrow.

Lord Jano sees Londo privately in his rooms. He tells him that the regent, who has been in seclusion for the last two months, has ordered that he be the only one allowed access to the status of the Centauri fleet, breaking from standard protocol without giving a reason. "It's a strange thing, Londo," Jano says. "As if darkness has fallen over the palace."

Jano returns to his rooms to find the lights not working. He takes a lamp from the side and turns to see the regent sitting in his chair. "If it were my decision, I would never let anyone harm you," the regent bumbles. "But it's not my decision, you see . . ." Jano turns and cries out, lifting his hands over his face as an unseen force throws him back against the wall and kills him.

Byron faces the council of the Interstellar Alliance to ask for a Homeworld to be provided for telepaths. He explains that his people have been secretly following all the ambassadors for two days, scanning every thought and every secret. "Give us a Homeworld of our own and you will never hear from us again," he asks. "Fail to do so and all of your secrets will be revealed."

Lyta gasps as she senses a Drazi slam his fist into the face of a human telepath. Then the other telepaths sense it, too. Byron urges them not to retaliate, but many of them remember another one of Byron's teachings—that they have to protect each other. They grab weapons and advance on the Drazi. Byron holds his head in his hands as he senses it all descending into brutal violence.

Londo runs in the darkened stone hallway while G'Kar turns to confront the three armed Centauri following them. "Mollari!" he calls out, as he hears the sound of stone grinding on stone. Londo tries to run back, but a slab falls and blocks his path, separating him from his bodyguard. He turns and finds Minister Vole is waiting for him. "You should never have come back to Centauri Prime," Vole says. "You are an obstacle to my ambitions." Vole draws a knife and throws it at Londo's chest. Londo steps back, but inexplicably, the knife hovers in the air just inches from his body. It turns, whips back toward Vole, and strikes him in the chest. Watching from the darkness are the glowing, red eyes of a Drakh.

Later that night, Londo finds the regent, who seems distracted, talking in riddles. "They like you, you know," he says. "That's why they saved you. They say you're just like them."

Sheridan withdraws his protection from the telepaths because of the violence, and those still loyal to Byron barricade themselves in Brown Sector. Lyta and Byron lie in bed, as Zack's warning comes over the public address system. "If you stay there and resist the order of the president . . . we cannot be held responsible for the consequences."

Some episodes are remembered by those who made them because they are such good stories, others are memorable for the guest actors, while still others are remembered for unexpected events that happen on the set. "In the Kingdom of the Blind" falls into the last category, at least for Patricia Tallman and Robin Atkin Downes. It was at this point that a flu virus that had been hanging around Los Angeles for some while decided to strike Robin down. "Robin got sick and took some cold medicine, some flu stuff so he could get [working]," Pat remembers. "Then he couldn't remember his lines! Because he never takes drugs, or aspirin, even. He doesn't do caffeine, he's a really pure spirit, so he takes his cold medicine and completely loses his mind! We're all going, 'Oh no.' It was horrible, poor baby, it was horrible for him."

Robin is slightly embarrassed to recall the episode. "Here we go!" he says, launching into the story. "The flu bug was going on, I think, when I started working on the show, and Pat and I managed to survive for a couple of months. Then I was coming up to shoot 'Kingdom of the Blind' and I was really sick. So the night before, I took some Contac and stuff you take for your cold, and it made me really airy. So the next day when I got on set I had one of these long speeches in front of the Alliance and I just kept going up on my lines. It was the first time I was blowing my lines and sweating all over the place. It was just frustrating. I don't think anything major happened, they managed to cut it together and I got all the lines out, but it was just a miserable experience."

This is somewhat of an interim episode for the telepath story line, bridging the gap as it does between the revelation of the Vorlons' hand in creating telepaths in "Secrets of the Soul" and the climax in "Phoenix Rising." But it is also an important episode because it is the beginning of the collapse of Byron's dream. Whereas Byron was able to largely keep the reins on his people in "Secrets of the Soul," here he begins to lose it. Even Byron secretly knew that his conviction toward nonviolence was not shared wholeheartedly by the others. He has to be around them, guiding them all the time to make sure they follow his way. When, in "Secrets of the Soul," his influence was taken away from them while he was locked in a holding cell, they killed a man. Here, the problem is taken one step further. It only took one telepath to disobey Byron, to leave the group for supplies when he had instructed them to stay out of sight, to provoke trouble. He was exposed right after Byron delivered his ultimatum to the Alliance and was vulnerable to the normals who were angry about their ambassadors being violated. The Drazi attack on that telepath spurs the other telepaths into action, and they take up weapons and resort to violence, thus shattering Byron's dream and bringing the inevitable clash between telepaths and normals that much closer.

Light years away, the other story line in the episode belongs to Londo and G'Kar. It is their first visit to Centauri Prime with the proud Narn as Londo's bodyguard. Here are two people who were at each other's throats at the beginning of *Babylon 5*'s grand arc, bitter enemies formed through a long and bloody history of war between their peoples. Since then, their individual stories have moved through two other wars toward some kind of resolution: G'Kar through his spiritual enlightenment and Londo through his apology to G'Kar. They have become, if not friends, then tolerant of each other. The irony is that G'Kar, who once dreamed of killing Londo, should now accompany him to Centauri Prime with the express purpose of protecting him from harm.

"It certainly wouldn't be possible for him to be his body-guard and to take what Delenn offered if it hadn't been for this change in the heart between the two of them—that it is on both sides," Andreas Katsulas, who plays G'Kar, says. "I think, more importantly, he does it out of a sense of commit-ment to the Alliance. I think he has the genuine conviction now that the good of the *whole* is what's going to benefit the *part*, the piece. So it is in his own people's best interest to do what is good for the whole. That's how he sees being Londo's bodyguard and everything else, so it's really opened up his horizons as to how to serve his people."

"An interesting twist," Peter Jurasik, who plays Londo, adds. "We have talked a couple of times about how Joe is looking for opportunities to push these characters together and keep them together. This was another plot device that ended up working really well, by sending this person to be his bodyguard, the absurdity of it, the wonder of it, the magic of it."

It is not appreciated by members of the Centauri court, of course, who find the idea of a Narn bodyguard totally abhor-rent, especially Minister Vitari, who seems convinced it must be a joke. "That was fun stuff to play," Peter says. "They found the haughtiest English actor they could find. We ended up with a wonderful actor named Neil Hunt, and I'm sure he's made a career out of saying [Peter adopts an upper-class English accent], 'Oh my goodness! Oh no who is that person? What is that smell? Remove that man!' I'm sure he's done that his whole career, but boy did he do it well, he was really terrific.

"It was an interesting episode and a fun one to do," Peter concludes. "Joe, in the fifth season, was able to go to some places where, if we'd had to roll and finish up the story line in [Season] Four, we never would have gotten to. G'Kar and Londo's story was really something else that he got to explore. He got to explore brand-new stuff with us, so hope-fully the fans will dig it. What is worrisome for me is the fact that in the fourth season they were so driven by the plot and loved the excitement of that, they may get into the fifth season and think, 'Oh this is all fluff, too superficial.' "

That was indeed the reaction of a handful of viewers, which provoked the following response from writer and executive producer J. Michael Straczynski: "The problem is on the one hand you have a lot of adrenaline junkies who think that unless there's a whole lot of stuff blowing up, nothing's happening, and those who think that unless they know in advance that this is an arc episode, it's not an arc episode, unless you telegraph it literally and they dismiss it. Without what's going on in the first half of the season, the major stuff that happens in the second half of the season won't matter, wouldn't play as well, and wouldn't have the same impact. They are part and parcel." [on the Internet]

"In the Kingdom of the Blind" is very clearly setting up events that will pay off further down the road. Zack's ultimatum over the public address system is an obvious flag leading into the confrontation that is to come in "Phoenix Rising" and to Lyta's change of heart, which dominates the latter third of the season. Wheels are also turning on Centauri Prime as the Drakh get closer to Londo and mark him as a valuable ally. The death of Jano, the assassination attempt on Londo, and the regent's ominous words that Londo is just like "them" combine to lay a sense of foreboding over Londo's fate. The fourth season had been able to tell its story at such a pace because it was delivering the payoff for things that had taken three years to set up. Now, in episodes like "In the Kingdom of the Blind," new elements and story lines are being set up once again, promising rewards just around the corner for those who would be patient.

9
"A Tragedy of Telepaths"

Cast

President John Sheridan ....Bruce Boxleitner
Michael Garibaldi ....Jerry Doyle
Delenn ....Mira Furlan
Zack Allan ....Jeff Conaway
Lyta Alexander ....Patricia Tallman
Londo Mollari ....Peter Jurasik
G'Kar ....Andreas Katsulas

Guest Stars

Byron ....Robin Atkin Downes
Worker ....Freddy Andreiuci
Na'Toth ....Julie Caitlin Brown
Lorg ....Caroline Ambrose
Drazi Ambassador ....Kim Strauss
Bezkiri Ambassador ....Jonathan Chapman
Guard ....Tom Billett
Bester ....Walter Koenig
Telepath #1 ....Christina Gavin
Thomas ....Leigh J. McCloskey

Londo and G'Kar open a cell door in a dark, almost forgotten part of the Centauri palace. They hear the sound of chains and find in the gloom, barely able to stand, G'Kar's former diplomatic attaché, Na'Toth.

G'Kar sits on the stone floor of the cell with Na'Toth as she recalls the devastation wrought on Narn in the war and her own capture. "I awoke in the ruins of the capital," she remembers. "A Centauri boot was on my throat . . . That's the last thing I remember until I woke up in a ship coming here." G'Kar turns to Londo and tells him that he must find a way to get her out of there.

The Drazi ambassador faces the Alliance council clutching a piece of metal found at the site of an attack on their ships. Analysis shows it to be of Brakiri origin. The Gaim ambassador stands holding his own piece of metal found at the site of an attack on Gaim ships. Analysis shows it to be of Drazi origin. Accusations fly across the council chamber, and Sheridan stands to try and calm them down. "Someone is hitting your people and leaving material that they hope will implicate the rest of you," he tells them. "Together we can figure this out." His words are enough to placate the angry voices, but not for long.

Londo has managed to smuggle Na'Toth out of the cell, but getting her on a transport to Babylon 5 is the difficult bit. G'Kar emerges from his quarters, with a dazed Na'Toth dressed as a Centauri woman leaning on his arm for support. Londo covers her face with a veil, takes her arm and a swig of liquor, and parades down the crowded hallway toward the transport in a drunken and raucous manner. Courtiers turn away, pretending not to see this example of debauchery swaying drunkenly past them, just as Londo had intended.

Bester stands alongside one of the entrances to Brown Sector that was welded shut by Byron's telepaths. His strong telepathic powers provide protection to the workman burning a hole through the metal so the rogues cannot enter his mind and make him stop. Then, suddenly, Zack cries "Down!" from nearby as he hears the sound of a PPG rifle power up. Bester dives out of the way and the PPG blast aimed at him strikes the workman instead. Security guards scatter and return fire at the group of rogue telepaths who attacked them. They soon withdraw, but leave two people dead. Inside the barricades, Byron realizes what is going on and looks to Lyta. "They're killing in my name," he says. "I have to stop it."

In fear of another attack, the Drazi have decided to keep their ships monitoring Brakiri ships, but Sheridan and Delenn have ordered the White Star fleet to monitor

Sheridan and the Alliance help to protect the Enfili from attacks in "The Paragon of Animals."

Maintenance men Bo and Mack get to witness a crisis first-hand in "A View from the Gallery."

John Sheridan with his wife Delenn and his ex-wife Elizabeth Lochley.

Franklin uncovers the Hyach's secrets in "Secrets of the Soul."

*Lyta is brought
closer to
switching her
allegiance to
Byron in
"Strange
Relations."*

*Byron is captured in
"Strange Relations."*

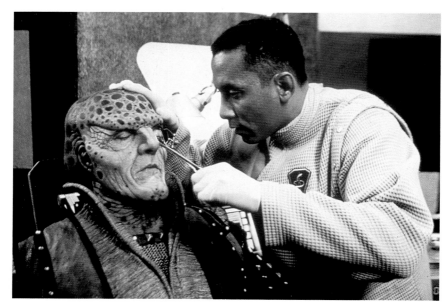

A new artificial eye for G'Kar in "Meditations on the Abyss."

A season of personal difficulties for Garibaldi (Jerry Doyle).

Zack ready for action in "Meditations on the Abyss."

Sheridan warns Lochley that the Centauri may attack Babylon 5 in "Movements of Fire and Shadow."

The Drakh reveals the keeper that will control Londo in "The Fall of Centauri Prime."

Sheridan and Delenn visiting the Centauri Palace in "The Fall of Centauri Prime."

Lennier's love for Delenn will lead to betrayal.

Sheridan passes beyond the rim in "Sleeping in Light."

them. They show this to the Drazi and Brakiri
ambassadors and promise to intervene if one attacks the
other. All that they want is to be given more time to
determine who is really behind the attacks. The Drazi
ambassador accepts it for the moment, but promises not
to forget that the Alliance threatened his people with
force.

Londo and G'Kar stand looking out of the window of
their transport, watching Na'Toth's ship sail away.
G'Kar reflects that it will take time for her spirit to heal.
"I have endured your cells," he says thoughtfully. "It
will be a long and difficult climb back into the light."

"I hope you'll like this one," actor Andreas Katsulas, who plays G'Kar, says. "I thought it was a great Londo and G'Kar episode. I think it's maybe one of my favorites from this season because I was pleased to see how G'Kar responds so emotionally to the situation of finding Na'Toth. Do you remember the movie *Ben Hur*? Do you remember when he finds his sister and his mother in the cave and they're lepers? It's that same total anguish where your heart breaks in a second. I remembered that image of the film and so by discovering Na'Toth after two years, when she should have been free all that time, sitting there and suffering and still wanting to be absolutely patriotic almost to the last breath when he tells her they won the war, I found it so touching that I really threw myself into that scene."

The episode saw the welcome return of Julie Caitlin Brown who—then going simply by the name "Caitlin Brown"—played the feisty Narn diplomatic attaché Na'Toth in the first season. Although the character was played briefly by Mary Kay Adams in the second year, it was Julie who really made the character her own and she who was asked to reprise the role. "When I went back on the show it was like I never left," she says. "It was lovely. I mean, the scenes we did were very emotional and revealed the depths of G'Kar's attachment to me and mine to him. The scenes I had with Andreas on the opening bit were some of the most dramatic scenes I have got to portray as an actor. And they were some of the most fulfilling because you really get to go there. You don't get to do that very often, not on television. I hope that Joe lets me come back and do one where I am not in such a depleted state because when I come back [in "A Tragedy of Telepaths"], you find out what happened to me over the last two years and it's some pretty bad stuff. I would like to come back as the old Na'Toth with that power again."

"A Tragedy of Telepaths" rounded off a question that had been hanging for three years—what happened to Na'Toth? It also brought a reminder of times past for Peter Jurasik, who, as Londo, got to fall about in a drunken state while trying to smuggle Na'Toth out of the Centauri palace. "That was so much fun to do again, I can't tell you," he says. "At this point I'm really done and finished with Londo, we've told the story and I'm kind of worn out. But if we had to go back, if someone pushed me out on stage and said, 'You've got to do Londo for five more episodes,' I would love to do the old Londo, the drunk Londo, the whoring, gambling Londo. He was fun. I've gotten so far away from that, so far afield from that guy that I would love to go back and do him again. There's a recklessness in the performance of it which is so much more fun, in some ways, to play because you just sort of jump off the diving board and jump into it. It was great to do that, to come around the corner drunk again and start grabbing at the Centauri women and be stumbling all over the place, loud, boisterous, and knocking into everyone and everything. It feels really random and volatile—it's great!"

The two other threads of the episode take place on Babylon 5. The business with the Drazi blaming the Brakiri for attacking their ships helps to keep that part of the story ticking over. The other arc is the telepath story line, from which the title of the episode comes. Most of it, such as the arrival of Bester and his Hounds, is a setup for the next episode, but there is also a building tension. While Byron is walled up inside Brown Sector with Security trying to get through to them from the outside, he does a surprising thing and invites Lochley to come and talk to him. He doesn't want to make demands or an ultimatum, he just wants to say good-bye as a matter of courtesy.

Lochley's journey to meet with him inside his self-built cell is a difficult one through a series of small maintenance ducts. It was one of the things that director Tony Dow had a clear vision of as soon as he read the script. "There's usually only a couple of images or a couple of sequences that I really get interested in, and I really focus on, and I try to have some control over," he says. "They're having to design and build the sets way in advance before I come on and start doing my prep, so I usually go in a couple of weeks in advance of that if there's something special that I would like. The conduit or the ducting that she was going through, I really wanted it to be tight because I've seen people go through ducts and they look kind of wide and it's evident that there's a lot of space. So we designed that thing to be very enclosed, and then we designed a special dolly, for lack of a better word. It looked like a pizza tray, a thing you get the pizza out of the oven with. It had a ten-foot-long handle, four little wheels, and we mounted the camera on that. Then we had the ducting, which had holes in it, so as the camera came back I could push objects in front of it so it would look like the camera had to get over these boxes and other things. It was just one of those things that I wanted to do so somebody would say, 'Wow, how did they do that?' "

"I enjoyed that," Tracy Scoggins, who had to crawl through it all, says. "I really enjoy doing physical things, so that was fun for me. I was crawling through this tight space, and at the end of the duct when I arrived at the location of the telepaths, it's kind of a high jump to jump down to the floor. I was a gymnast and a springboard diver, so I hung onto the pipe and swung down. The director goes, 'Oh, that's great, this time swing out farther and then crouch down,' and we did it that way, and then he goes, 'This time drop over in the corner.' And I said, 'Wait, I'm starting to feel like Frances Farmer here, okay?' [Frances Farmer was an actress from the 1930s; the 1982 film *Frances* includes a sequence where a movie director keeps making her fall over in a patch of mud.]

"It was fun, I enjoy doing the physical things, and I like that about Lochley. Any person in command could have said,

'Okay, soldier, get on into that duct and get on to the telepaths,' but that's not Lochley. She's hands-on and I like that about her, that she's not afraid, that her courage extends into her physical realm."

But the pleasant exchanges between Byron and Lochley are all over when Bester appears and the tension increases. With Byron trapped inside, he is both a sitting duck for the Psi Cop and separated from his former followers outside who want to fight in his name. Bereft of his influence, they brutally attack security guards and steal weapons in order to strike back at Bester.

This was another thing Tony Dow wanted to make sure was right. "What I was concerned about in that show was the violence," he said. "I remember the first fight thing I did on *Babylon 5* in Season Four ["Atonement"]. I'm not much for blood and stuff and I don't like gratuitous violence at all, and I remember shying away from having something very graphic. Then when I saw it I was a little disappointed because it really didn't have the punch that it should have had. So with this script, I went as far as I could with the violence. I was saying to the assistant director, or I'd get [producer] John Copeland and say, 'Hey, come down and take a look at this. Do we have too much blood?' I think in my cut it was pretty violent, I had it pretty strong and pretty realistic."

The episode was originally called "Cat and Mouse" in reference to the moves and countermoves played between Byron, Bester, and Zack. Writer and executive producer J. Michael Straczynski explains the first title was just a working title that became useful in disguising some of the upcoming story lines, so he kept it for quite some time, including during production. In the end, though, it was decided to name the episode "A Tragedy of Telepaths" instead. "I figured, a flock of geese, a herd of buffalo, a tragedy of telepaths . . . Actually, though, the credit for that must go to John Copeland who came up with it over lunch one day."

10
"Phoenix Rising"

Cast
President John Sheridan ....Bruce Boxleitner
Michael Garibaldi ....Jerry Doyle
Dr. Stephen Franklin ....Richard Biggs
Captain Elizabeth Lochley ....Tracy Scoggins
Zack Allan ....Jeff Conaway
Lyta Alexander ....Patricia Tallman

Guest Stars
Byron ....Robin Atkin Downes
Peter ....Jack Hannibal
Telepath ....Victor Love
Thomas ....Leigh J. McCloskey
Bester ....Walter Koenig

"Turn around very, very slowly." Bester does so, to see Garibaldi pointing a PPG right at him. He wants Bester to admit, on record, that he conditioned him to betray Sheridan. Bester refuses and Garibaldi lifts the PPG higher, aiming it right between his eyes. "I don't care if I go up for your murder or not. Not after what you did to me." He wills his finger to squeeze the trigger, his body shakes, but he cannot fire. Bester smiles self-assuredly. There is a neural block in Garibaldi's mind—he cannot kill Bester no matter how much he wants to.

Byron was once Bester's protégé. A strong P12, he had no choice but to join the Psi Corps, where he tracked down rogues and was ordered to fire on a ship of mundanes who were helping them escape. He pulled the trigger, but afterwards left the Corps. "I swore I'd never allow innocents to be harmed like that again," he tells Lyta. "Swore to find a better way for us, for our people, without violence."

But on one of the levels above him, a group of Byron's telepaths are charging Medlab with PPG rifles.

Garibaldi punches several as they come streaming through the door, firing PPG blasts that make medical staff scatter. Franklin steps in to help with his fists, but he is beaten back, knocked dizzy by a punch to the face, and he slumps to the floor. Meanwhile, Garibaldi struggles uselessly against the grip of several telepaths. "Unless we get what we want," says their leader, Thomas, "they're all dead."

Lyta puts her hand on an access panel and searches the air duct with her mind, swooping down lengths of tubing-laced tunnels until she reaches a dead end. She tries another and then another before finding a way through. She and Byron climb inside.

Sheridan refuses to bargain with the telepaths and offers them an ultimatum: either they surrender or he will use force to get them out. Thomas takes it as a signal to start killing the hostages and turns to Garibaldi, powering up his PPG. Garibaldi tenses at the sound and gunfire shoots across Medlab, knocking Thomas to the ground. They all turn to see Byron holding a PPG, the guilt of what he has just done written on his face.

Byron and the others stand in a hallway in Down Below, ready to surrender to Sheridan in return for allowing the ones who were not responsible for the violence to leave. But Bester's men come running round the corner and the rogues panic. "No!" one of the telepaths cries. "I won't go back with them!" He pulls out his PPG and fires. The corridor is suddenly full of gunfire. A security guard is hit and crashes against a pipe, knocking its cap off and causing a chemical to leak onto the floor. Byron steps forward and cries out, but is struck in the arm by a PPG blast. Lochley seizes the shock of the moment to order everyone to cease fire. In the sudden quiet, Byron picks up a PPG in front of him. "We can't go back now, there's too much blood," he says. He embraces Lyta for the last time and urges her to leave. As she walks away, Byron raises the PPG.

*Sheridan and Bester's men run while Byron's telepaths
gather around him. He pulls the trigger and the chemical
spill erupts into a ball of flame that engulfs them all.*

   *Garibaldi stares at a glass of liquor on the table in his
quarters. He raises it to his lips, pours it down his
throat, and savors its warmth. He twists the empty glass
in his hand, staring thoughtfully as it catches the light.*

Season Five's tough six-day-per-episode shooting schedule proved too tough for "Phoenix Rising." "When we
first got the script I remember reading it and thinking there's
too much stuff to do here in six days," director David Eagle
recalls. "Before I had a chance to even talk to John Copeland about it, Pam Eillerson, who's the first AD, called me up
and said, 'Have you read the script yet? Do you believe how
much stuff we have to do? I'm not sure it can be done in six
days.' I said, 'I'm glad you think that way because that's how
I feel.' " They both talked to producer John Copeland, who
agreed the episode was a special case and deserved an
extra day. It became the only one of the season to be filmed
in seven days. "Even with seven days it was not a simple
matter," David continues. "There's a huge scene at the end
with about a hundred extras where Byron and most of the
rest of the telepaths get blown up, so it was pretty big."

   Several story lines come together to make this the most
significant episode of the season so far. The telepaths provide the focus for the episode, of course, but it is also the
chance for Garibaldi to finally confront Bester. "That's one of
the best scenes I've had in all the years that I've done this
show as far as I'm concerned," Walter Koenig, who plays
Bester, says. "I loved that scene! I may be showing a lack of
humility, but I loved that scene. That was a good show, it was
really a fast-moving, strong show."

   This moment had been teased out as long as it possibly
could. After waiting so long to settle the score, having been
denied the opportunity by Lochley during Bester's previous
visit, Garibaldi is now ready to taste revenge. He does it the
simple way by taking a gun and breaking into Bester's room.

But something bothered actor Jerry Doyle about the scene when he first read it. "He turns his back and I sneak up on him in this room and all the lights were on—where was I hiding? In the closet? Under the sink?"

He decided to play it as if Garibaldi had no intention of hiding, that he was just sitting there calmly waiting for Bester to arrive. "Then I said to him, 'You have to sense that I'm in the room, that will help me,' " Jerry continues. " 'Then when you turn to me, if you play that you think I'm going to kill you even though you know that I can't, that's going to give the scene a whole different twist.' If I've got the gun and he plays casual because he knows that I can't do it, that would have given it away, the audience would be saying, 'What's up? There's something up.' But this way, Garibaldi was relaxed, he [Bester] was afraid, which was the way the scene looked. Then when the twist came, the reverse took over—he got casual and I got pissed."

All Garibaldi can do to take out his frustration is fire into the Babcom unit, but this is not the end of the issue for him. Garibaldi has been messed with once by Bester, and the neural block that prevents him from killing the Psi Cop is being messed with all over again. His first move is to seek out Dr. Franklin to find out about beating neural blocks, but this just gets him into a whole lot more trouble when the telepaths storm Medlab and take him hostage. Being beaten up and almost killed in the name of their cause pushes him the last step over the edge. He gives up on any attempt to look for a way to combat the neural block and reaches for the bottle. But this is no sudden impulse. He goes shopping, buys alcohol, brings it back to his quarters, then contemplates it before downing the glass. This is a deliberate decision to seek refuge in booze, knowing, as an alcoholic, exactly what it will do to him.

The scene where Garibaldi is almost shot is a repetition of the scene in the last episode of Season Four, "The Deconstruction of Falling Stars." Then, it was a glimpse into the future, a hint of what troubles lay around the corner for Babylon 5. Now, the scene gets the opportunity to be played out in full. "We had to look at that and re-create what the Medlab looked like in that scene from 'Deconstruction' and then work backwards," David Eagle says. "We had to put the lab back together in such a way that after all these people had charged in and shot people up and had hand-to-hand combat, it looked like what the Medlab looked like in 'Deconstruction.' That was a challenge doing that."

The fight itself was the first one to feature Richard Biggs as Dr. Franklin following his accident the previous year. In "Between the Darkness and the Light" he had accidentally punched a stuntman and almost took out his eye. Coincidentally, that was also an episode directed by David Eagle. "It's a running joke," David says. "I used to kid Rick every show I did. [I'd say,] 'Joe's decided to write in another fight scene for you because you were so effective in the last one!' So we always kid around about that and say, 'Here's a show where he's really in a fight scene and we couldn't get any stuntmen who wanted to do it with him, and certainly not the guy he knocked out!'—but that wasn't really true, that was just a thing we joke about. And he was really quite good, he did the fight scene perfectly, he never hurt anybody. He didn't get hurt. No one got hurt."

"In some episodes the doctor just isn't in a fighting mood and then in other episodes he becomes a world boxer kind of a guy," Rick Biggs reflects. "But he definitely can hold his own when needed. I think Joe is constantly trying to get me out of the cerebral, doctor kind of mentality, and the more physical I am, it shows another side of the doctor. In 'Phoenix Rising' they had me fighting, but I lost the fight to a girl. A girl beat me up in Medlab!"

The events in Medlab are what finally bring the situation surrounding Byron and his followers to a head. This is a man who came aboard Babylon 5 like some kind of Gandhi figure, with the trigger that had turned him into such an idealistic and passionate man hidden in his past. The only clues to go on were hints of a previous relationship with Bester. It is something he is ashamed of, something he does not want to talk about, but something that Lyta persuades out of him.

And, as he recounts his time as a Psi Cop, we see a flash-back of him in a Black Omega Starfury at the moment he killed a ship full of mundanes.

"It's really strange because you're actually standing up," Robin Atkin Downes says, remembering filming that scene in the cockpit. "You're standing up in the Starfury and you're trying to keep your head straight. You're enjoying it because you know what it's going to look like when it comes out, but it's kind of unreal when you're standing up there, you're holding yourself up like you're squatting over a toilet bowl or something. Then you've got the big helmet on so it's hard to hear the direction when they say 'action' to get the timing right—but I was real excited to be in the Omega ship. It was exciting, it felt like Luke Skywalker. I was in my flight suit and it was just fun."

Understanding what made Byron choose to lead his group of telepaths toward a better life helps explain why, at the end, he is willing to make the ultimate sacrifice for the cause he believes in. He leaves behind only two things—his legacy, and Lyta to continue his work.

"It was terrible, it was really terrible," actress Patricia Tallman says. "Lyta's supposed to walk away, and Joe and I had been arguing back and forth about this. I said, 'I can't do it, I can't do it.' He said, 'Well, she has to do it and then it changes her,' and I said, 'But how am I supposed to do that?' How do you effectively walk away from the person you love when you know they're about to destroy themselves? I just didn't know how I could do that. Even to the moment of shooting, I didn't know how we were going to do that. He actually rewrote a bit for me to give me a little more leading into it and explain a little more, but he never changed his mind. He held tight to what he felt was important to what was going on."

"For me it was the most intense episode," Robin con-cludes. "Not only was it coming up to the end of Byron's journey, but it was the end of my journey at *Babylon 5*, working there and getting to work on this incredible role. It was all coming to an end. Then the day that we shot the last scene where I blow up everybody including myself was really intense. We worked that scene from seven-thirty in the morning to eight at night and we didn't get to our closeups until the end of the day. Pat and I were really emotionally drained. It was definitely a day to remember, one I won't forget."

11
"Day of the Dead"

Cast

President John Sheridan ....Bruce Boxleitner
Michael Garibaldi ....Jerry Doyle
Delenn ....Mira Furlan
Captain Elizabeth Lochley ....Tracy Scoggins
Lennier ....Bill Mumy
Londo Mollari...Peter Jurasik
G'Kar ....Andreas Katsulas

Guest Stars

Rebo and Zooty ....Penn and Teller
Lt. David Corwin ....Josh Cox
Zoe ....Bridget Flanery
Dodger ....Marie Marshall
Adira Tyree ....Fabiana Udenio
Morden ....Ed Wasser
Brakiri Ambassador ....Jonathan Chapman
ISN Reporter ....Mary Major
Customs Officer ....Skip Stellrecht
Brakiri Salesman ....Ismael Kanater

A crowd has gathered in the Rotunda to see the almost legendary comedy duo Rebo and Zooty. "Ladies and Gentlemen," Rebo begins. "Mr. President, alien races with ears, alien races without ears, and Zooty's friend Bingo the Invisible Fish." Everyone finds this hysterically funny, except for Lochley, who is less than impressed. She sneaks away to a meeting she has with the Brakiri ambassador. He wants to buy a part of the station for the night for a religious festival called the "Day of the Dead."

The festival has so intrigued Lennier that he has returned to Babylon 5 to experience it. Garibaldi, on the other hand, couldn't care less. He steps over the chalk line that separates Brakiri territory from Babylon 5, brushing aside the Brakiri ambassador who is trying to explain it to him.

The lights go out in Londo's quarters, leaving nothing but the pale red glow of the emergency lighting. He turns and sees the beautiful figure of a young Centauri woman in the half-light. "Adira? Adira Tyree?" he says, looking at his murdered lover, inexplicably standing before him. He takes her hand and kisses it, overcome by joyous laughter. "I am to be emperor; I am the savior of our people," he tells her. "But I think that I would give it all away to have you back."

Garibaldi's eyes flicker awake as he hears the sound of the shower. He reaches under his pillow for his PPG and stalks round to the bathroom. He stops agog at finding a naked woman—Dodger, the marine he once almost went to bed with. His mind tumbles, deciding it must be some kind of Psi Corps trick. "It's no one's dirty little trick," Dodger says, lounging provocatively on his bed. "Happy Day of the Dead."

Lochley hears coughing and turns to see a thin, wan, teenage girl standing in her quarters. "Zoe?" she says, tears welling in her eyes. "Oh my God, Zoe." Twenty years ago she had found Zoe on the floor of their bathroom, covered in cockroaches, having choked to death on her own vomit. They are painful memories, and Zoe doesn't want to dwell on the past for too long. She wants to party and asks Lochley if she has any "stuff." But Lochley gave all that up years ago. "You don't party?" Zoe says. "Jeez, Lizzie, what did you grow up to be?"

Lennier springs from his meditation and extends his fighting pike, thrusting it toward the man who has suddenly appeared in his quarters—Morden. "You like being a Ranger, Lennier?" the former servant of the Shadows asks. "Would you like it any better if I were to tell you that you will betray the Anla'shok?" But Lennier does not believe his prophecy. This was not the wisdom he was expecting from the dead.

*Lennier turns, but Morden is gone. The newspaper he
was reading flutters harmlessly to the floor.*

*Garibaldi laughs with Dodger as they sing Emily
Dickinson poems to the tune of "The Yellow Rose of
Texas." Then her expression becomes distant. She kisses
him lightly on the forehead, gets up, and walks away,
leaving Garibaldi humming the tune thoughtfully to
himself.*

*Zoe senses something and takes hold of Lochley's
hand. "I do remember my death," she says earnestly.
"I didn't want to hurt you. But yeah, I did do it on
purpose . . . Don't hate me." Zoe's hand pulls away and
she is gone.*

*Lochley tells Sheridan that the whole night is a
mystery and that she was told to give him a message
from someone called Kosh: "When the Long Night
comes, return to the End of the Beginning."*

It was only after the script was written that it seemed like a
good idea to cast a genuine comedy duo as Rebo and
Zooty. Penn and Teller, comedy magicians who have become
famous through numerous, and often adult, TV appearances,
seemed to fit the bill. They said yes and were hired. The
script was then adapted to allow Teller to stay within character by not speaking. Any dialogue he had was transferred
to his "machine" and was voiced by the ever-versatile
Babylon 5 creative consultant Harlan Ellison.

Rebo and Zooty were first mentioned in Season Four's
"Rumors, Bargains and Lies" in an apparently throwaway
joke where Londo complains to Sheridan about the peculiari-
ties of human psychology. "The less said about the comedy
team of Rebo and Zooty, the better." And on the evidence of
their comedy routine in "Day of the Dead," he would appear
to have a point. But clearly the twenty-third century has different tastes than the twentieth because they are a big hit
on Babylon 5, with everyone finding them hysterical . . . well,
almost everyone.

"Oh my God," Bruce Boxleitner says, looking a little

uncomfortable about being asked what it was like to work with Penn and Teller. "They aren't my favorite comedians. I don't want to say anything bad, but it's not my brand of humor. They were a bit abusive. Whoever the little guy was [Teller], he was rather good. Whoever the other guy was, he was rather arrogant beyond belief. He kind of looked at us kind of like, 'What am I doing this kind of stuff for?' But they certainly answered the bill for the episode and that's what counts. I did my Rebo and Zooty impression the year before, so I guess I had to finally see where it came from. I liked mine better."

Mira Furlan, however, had a totally different reaction. "I loved them. I want to see them," she says. "I bonded with Penn. He asked me, 'You're from Yugoslavia? You must have listened to a lot of Zapper.' And I said, 'How did that come to you?' because I really did, I was a big Zapper fan when I was very young. And he just has this very irreverent mind. He has a lot of interesting points on freedom. We spoke about the First Amendment, we spoke about the Constitution of the United States, and it was interesting for me, very interesting, I really admired him. But I'm totally unfamiliar with their work, everyone knew who they were except me. So I have to fill that void in my education and go and see Penn and Teller."

The script for "Day of the Dead" is the only one not to have been written by J. Michael Straczynski this season. In fact, you have to go back as far as the second season and Lawrence G. DiTillio's "Knives" to find an episode by another writer. After the grueling effort of writing two whole seasons on his own, Joe Straczynski had vowed in a state of virtual exhaustion that he would not be doing so again—but Neil Gaiman was the only outside writer to contribute a script.

Joe had known Neil Gaiman for some time, not only as a person, but also through his work, most notably on the *Sandman* comics. By this stage, British-born Neil had also written his own television series, *Neverwhere*, a fantasy drama set underneath London, for the BBC in the U.K. It made for an easy relationship between writer and executive producer. "I get involved to different degrees with different writers," Joe explains. "With Neil, it was more 'What do you want to write?' He noodled around with some ideas, ran one past me that he liked, and I liked it. He asked for a truckload of scripts for reference, picked the characters he wanted to use, researched them, we talked on the phone and via e-mail a number of times as he refined his ideas further, then he wrote the script. I tucked and nipped a little here and there, but pretty much left it alone." [on the Internet]

One of the characters Neil chose to use was Lennier, who had been temporarily absent from Babylon 5 on Ranger training. When he returned, he came back in a Ranger uniform which, it has to be said, is a great little outfit. "I like it too," actor Bill Mumy says. "When I was four years old I sat with a broken leg and stared at Guy Williams' Zorro and George Reeves' Superman and that's what inspired me to want to be in television. So here I am almost forty years later—I finally got my cape!"

Lennier had hoped to gain wisdom during the Day of the Dead festival, but what he found, he didn't like. The figure who returns from the dead to see him is the Shadows' associate Morden. A surprising choice. "You would think that Marcus would have come back to Lennier, or Morden would have come to someone else," Bill says. "But it's an interesting episode. I'm a big Neil Gaiman fan, and Neil and I have chatted at various comic book stores and stuff, so it was nice to work with Neil's words for a change—and to have Neil include Lennier in his script was a compliment."

The other unearthly visitors are more predictable. For Londo, it is Adira, the woman he once loved and then lost when Morden had her killed. But before actor Peter Jurasik can be drawn to talk about working with actress Fabiana Udenio again, he takes time to mention an earlier scene with a Brakiri salesman. It is essentially a setting-up, exposition scene, but it clearly made an impression on Peter. "God, I had such a good time doing this scene. This particular actor [Ismael Kanater], it was quite extraordinary for me to be in a scene with someone where I actually wondered if he was an alien or not. He seemed so otherworldly. The way he approached the language, the way he spoke, even when he spoke to me when the camera wasn't rolling, made me wonder whether he was even from our world. I'm not necessarily one to entertain that kind of fancy, but this particular guy—man, what a performance! He struggled with the language in just the right way so that he was a foreigner and had a mannerism about his body so that I just loved his performance. There are a couple of other performances I've noted before, Clive Revill [Trakis in Season One's "Born to the Purple"] and a couple of other of my favorites, but this guy—gee, he was wonderful!"

The scenes with Adira were just one additional pleasure. "All I had to do that particular day was get into my Londo pajamas and get kissed. Wow! What a day! Jerry Doyle always talks about his favorite day being when he was flat on his back and unconscious [in Season Two's "Points of Departure"], but this would best those days. When you crawl into bed and have a pretty girl crawl on top of you and kiss you and they're actually paying you—it's a good day at work, I've gotta tell you! That was a lot of fun. She's a wonderful actress, too, by the way. I raved about the other guy, but she really is very sweet and very studied. The quality they were trying to get with Adira was that she would be a slave girl, but not be at all whorish and not so sickeningly sweet, and Fabiana really captured that."

A lover of a different kind comes back to Garibaldi. Dodger, before she died, wanted one last fling before going into battle and was turned down by Garibaldi. Her return gives him a second chance. "When I first read the thing about she and I being in bed and doing whatever, I wanted to have it play out like the morning after in *Casablanca*—did they or didn't they?" actor Jerry Doyle says. "I wanted to leave that up to the audience. I say they didn't, other people say they did, and hopefully we'll never know."

But probably the most moving sequences are those between Lochley and Zoe, as the tough EarthForce captain faces some of her own vulnerability with the return of someone who was once a soul mate. There are glimpses of her teenage life, a rebellion against her military father, and her escape into an ugly drug culture. At the heart of it are her feelings for Zoe, her best friend that she found dead and covered in cockroaches in her bathroom. It reawakens painful memories for Lochley and evoked an emotional performance from actress Tracy Scoggins. "At the end of the day your heart doesn't feel like you were doing it for money," she says. "You really feel like you were *there* again because, to make it real, you use certain sense memories. It took a lot out of me, but I really enjoyed it."

12
"The Ragged Edge"

Cast

President John Sheridan ....Bruce Boxleitner
Michael Garibaldi ....Jerry Doyle
Delenn ....Mira Furlan
Dr. Stephen Franklin ....Richard Biggs
Zack Allan...Jeff Conaway
Londo Mollari...Peter Jurasik
G'Kar ....Andreas Katsulas

Guest Stars

Brannagan ....Mirron E. Willis
Ta'Lon ....Marshall Teague
Tafiq Azir ....John Castellanos
Narn #1 ....Mark Hendrickson

An energy blast strikes Redstar 9, destroying one of the ship's cargo pods. Inside, Brannagan wrestles with the controls, but the attack is too intense. He heads for the lifepod as a blast strikes the hull, igniting a series of explosions. The lifepod gently sails away and, behind it, Redstar 9 is destroyed in a ball of flame.

Londo and G'Kar have arrived back on Babylon 5, but every time G'Kar walks past another Narn, the Narn bows toward him. G'Kar bows back, rather puzzled.

G'Kar is delighted when he sees his old friend Ta'Lon back on the station, but less than delighted when he hears that Ta'Lon "liberated" the book G'Kar had been writing from his quarters. However, that is nothing compared to his anger when he hears it has been copied and is now being treasured as a holy book by almost every Narn on the station. "Congratulations, Citizen G'Kar," Ta'Lon says. "You are now a religious icon."

Garibaldi arrives on the Drazi Homeworld, in search of Brannagan, the Human pilot who survived the attack on his ship and could provide a clue as to who was behind the attack. He steps out onto the huge balcony of his hotel room and takes in the splendor of the city beneath him. Then he hears a sound behind him and his hand dives automatically into his jacket where he powers up a PPG. He swivels and points his PPG at the man, then, after a moment, he relaxes and hugs his old friend, Tafiq. Tafiq sets two glasses and a bottle of liquor on the table. "No, I don't . . ." Garibaldi begins, then changes his mind and lets his friend pour him a drink.

Tafiq empties the bottle of booze and glances over to Garibaldi, asleep on the balcony. He leaves, a little drunkenly, to make their travel arrangements. In the corridor, someone calls his name and he turns just in time to see a Drazi shoot him in the chest. Tafiq collapses in the corridor while, inside, Garibaldi is still sleeping.

Garibaldi bends down over his friend. "The pilot," Tafiq gasps, between breaths. "You have to get to him . . . before they do." Garibaldi helplessly watches the life slip out of Tafiq, then runs.

Turning the corner of a narrow street, he sees three cloaked figures standing above a human body. Garibaldi yells and charges at them, firing his PPG. He hits one with a plasma blast, another of them with his fist, but their reflexes are better than his and they punch and kick him to the floor, leaving him alone and semiconscious.

Back on Babylon 5, Garibaldi tells the others what happened. He is clutching a button, the only thing he managed to bring back from the trip. Londo arrives late to the meeting and takes the button from his hand. He recognizes the design as belonging to the Imperial guards at the Centauri royal court. The others exchange glances, suddenly realizing it is the Centauri who are behind the attacks. Londo doesn't sense their changed mood and hands back the button, totally unaware of the gravity of what he has just told them.

Franklin walks into Sheridan's office, a look of seriousness on his face. He has been offered a job, a good job back on Earth, and although he will miss

*Babylon 5, he has decided to take it. "I wanted you to
be the first to know," he says to Sheridan, taking a deep
breath. "Effective January 1, 2263, I'll be the new head
of xenobiological research at EarthDome."*

"The Ragged Edge" is *Babylon 5*'s one hundredth episode, an important point in marking the show's longe-
vity. The story itself is no special celebration of this fact, but
the episode became important as the show looked toward
the future.

When producer John Copeland was asked which episodes
he would like to direct this season, the first one he chose
was production number 513—Season Five, episode 13—
which later became known as "The Ragged Edge." Writer
J. Michael Straczynski was anticipating this would be the
end of the telepath arc and probably a big episode. In
the end, the climax of that story came in "Phoenix Rising,"
but John Copeland wasn't bothered too much. He had
chosen the episode purely because he likes the number thirteen. "I was born on Friday 13," he explains. "If it's up to me
to pick any number, I'll always pick thirteen first."

This is the first time *Babylon 5* has visited the Drazi
Homeworld, and it is somewhat of a rare outing for the show.
After all, the original plan that sold the show in the first place
was that the stories would largely be set onboard the space
station—and hence not run up uncontrollable expenses by
roaming around the galaxy. Occasional exceptions were
made, like the trips to Centauri Prime, but those expenses
were justified because they are locations that are used over
and over again. Going to the Drazi Homeworld was different
because it's only featured in two episodes. But rather than
being a one-off, it was hoped that this short visit to a different planet would set the pattern for the planned spin-off
series *Crusade* in which the characters regularly move from
one planet to another.

"We're going to be visiting a lot of different, varied types
of locations, and this is something we have mulled around
for quite a while," says John. "What we felt we wanted to
try was to not do what everybody else has done. This is not

just *Star Trek* or *Space: 1999* or *Space: Above and Beyond*. Whenever they do a location on another planet, they go out to Vasquez Rocks [in Southern California]. I mean it's been in a million westerns over the years, it's been in many episodes of *Star Trek*, it's featured in *Starship Troopers*. We didn't want to go to places that are going to look like Earth, so what we attempted to do—and this was really our first attempt on 'The Ragged Edge'—was to try to create a virtual location that felt and looked different and had a different quality of light and all that. For a first step at doing this kind of thing, I think we were pretty good. There were a few miscommunications that happened on our effects stuff, so we need to coordinate that a little bit better, but overall I think what the audience will come away with after watching it is, it really is a different place."

In order to be as authentic as possible—or as one can be with a fictional alien planet—John called Inge Heyer, their friendly expert at the Hubble Space Telescope project, and told her everything Joe had told him about the planet: it orbits at roughly the same distance from its blue-white star as Earth does around the Sun, and it has a yellowish atmosphere because of the particulates in the air, generated by industry among other things. "[I said,] 'Now, given those parameters, what color's the sunset?' Because here where we have a blue sky because of all the water vapor, our sunsets tend to be red and gold. On Mars, which has a red atmosphere, the sunset is actually a deep blue. So they came back and gave us the wavelengths of colors and we translated that into what the lighting gels would be, and it's an amber and yellowish green light on the Drazi Homeworld.

"We also wanted to make it kind of hot and steamy, and I think it worked pretty well. I think also when Jerry walks out onto the balcony of his hotel room and the city spreads out beneath him, that's a pretty spectacular shot. This tells me we can successfully create these environments here. We want things to look alien, we're going to want them to look like they are not on Earth, therefore there's no location that you can go out to outside and create that kind of stuff. Even if you put a graduated filter in front of the camera lens, which is what they did with *Space: Above and Beyond* and a few other things, it looks like a sky in a music video! You're not kidding anybody. So we really want to create illusions. I think, to me, that's what our job is, to create and sustain an illusion without having to make it real."

The visit to the Drazi Homeworld was a pretty physical one for Jerry Doyle as Garibaldi. He's fighting in almost every scene, and not just simple fights either. His encounter with a Drazi, whom he ends up tipping over the balcony, was a long, brutal, bloody fight. Then when he meets the hooded Centauri outside in the street he is virtually beaten up. "It was a fun episode," Jerry says. "I remember there was a lot of fighting and running and diving and shooting. I had to run down a hall, hit a trampoline, fly across the room, crash into these guys. It was kinda cool."

Storywise, the point of this roughing up is partly so he picks up a vital clue to implicate the Centauri as the perpetrators of the attacks on shipping lanes. More importantly it's to open up Garibaldi's weaknesses. The old Garibaldi would have not got himself into a position where he had to flee the planet almost empty-handed. The old Garibaldi would not have continued sleeping while his friend was killed in the corridor outside. But this Garibaldi, the drunken Garibaldi, does just that. "I think there's a lot of pressure on him," Jerry says, explaining his character's reasons for going back to the bottle. "Also, things are starting to get really good, so you've got to test it. I got a good job, I got a nice relationship, things are going good, then when you think you can handle things, that's when you introduce things that you shouldn't. Then you go into denial, and the consequences of his actions this year, as opposed to the first year when he went off the wagon, are much greater. War ensues, people die. In the first season he was just hurting himself and screwing up a relationship or two, but in this it's a much higher consequence: the friendships that have been made, the bonds that have been established. What I liked about it was it wasn't a one-episode 'Oh, he's drinking again—oh he's not,' like it was in the first season. This really played out for six or seven episodes and gave me a chance to work with it."

Meanwhile, on the station, wheels are slowly turning in the lives of two others. For G'Kar, it is the consequences of writing about his spiritual transformation in the book now known by every Narn on the station as *The Book of G'Kar*. He had not intended for it to be published before his death, but now that it has been he shies away from the adulation of those who have read it, even though his teachings are getting a wider hearing. "He, I think, is quite wise in seeing the danger that people will be adoring the person and not the message that they're spreading," Andreas Katsulas, who plays G'Kar, says. "People begin to immediately trivialize and make a circus out of things that were in a true state at one time, and I think that he recognizes that what he found for himself, people can also find out for themselves. But it won't be by any form of imitation or idolatry, it's just work that you have to do."

For Dr. Franklin, it is an offer of a better job back on Earth. It is a tough decision to leave, but he cannot turn down such an opportunity. He begins a trend that many of the characters will follow as the season continues, of leaving behind the past and setting out on a new direction. For actor Richard Biggs, it became somewhat of a mirror of his own situation. "That was a first moment, as far as Richard Biggs was confronted with, of actually having to deal with leaving the show and putting into words how I am going to do this," he says. "So not only was Franklin leaving, but also I think that was the first stage of me going, 'Hey this is it, I can see the end of the tunnel.' I think it affected me much sooner than everyone else because my character had to deal with it so much sooner than anyone else's. Everyone else was still in the middle of the fifth year and still not knowing what's going on, and I knew that after 522 I would be getting on a plane and heading on out."

13
"The Corps Is Mother, the Corps Is Father"

Cast

Dr. Stephen Franklin ....Richard Biggs
Zack Allan ....Jeff Conaway

Guest Stars

Lauren Ashley ....Dana Barron
Drake ....Mike Genovese
Chen Hikaru ....Reggie Lee
Jonathan Harris ....Dex Elliott Sanders
Bester ....Walter Koenig
Gordon ....Brendan Ford
Bartender ....Don McMillan
Man ....Jeremy Thomas
Roommate ....Michael Max Charles Ciano
Dealer ....Michael Jeffrie Stanton
Bryce ....Vince Ricotta

Assistant Director Drake of the Psi Corps greets Alfred Bester as he walks into his office in the Martian headquarters and introduces him to two young interns. Lauren and Chen stand nervously. Bester is to show them the ropes over the next couple of days.

Bester's tour of the facilities is interrupted by a message from Drake. One of his students has been found dead; murdered, presumably by his roommate Jonathan Harris. Drake assigns Bester to the case, but before he and his interns can leave, Drake takes him aside and warns him that Harris was being trained in attack probes. "He's a mind-shredder, Al. Let him get too close . . . and he'll rip you in two."

Bester follows Harris' trail to Babylon 5, and five hours later a body is discovered. The dead man worked in the casino. There seems to be no reason why Harris would have picked this particular man to kill, until Zack tells him Harris has been seen on a rather successful gambling spree, unusual for a telepath unpracticed in gambling. It seems that Harris ripped the knowledge out of the man's mind before he died.

Chen spots Harris in the smoky, crowded Happy Daze bar. Chen slips out into the corridor, looking for a BabCom unit. He starts to record a message for Bester, then senses someone behind him. He turns too late to stop a knife being plunged into his chest. Chen sinks to the floor, dead.

Zack plays back the snatch of the recording, freezing it at the moment Chen was stabbed. The hand holding the knife has a distinctive tattoo—but it is not Harris'.

The tattooed hand, belonging to a man named Bryce, takes a handful of money from Harris. It's his ten percent for helping the telepath get enough cash to get away. But Bryce wants to know why. What is he running from? "I don't know," Harris says. "I'm not even sure how I got here. One minute I was in the testing center and the next . . . I don't remember!"

With Chen gone, Bester and Lauren are left to figure out the puzzle by themselves. Bester looks through Harris' papers, but they seem to be jumbled, written by different people in different handwriting, using different names. Then Lauren finds something: a recording of one of Harris' scanning and blocking training sessions. Suddenly, in the middle of the exercise, Harris leaps out of his chair. His partner tries to calm him down, but Harris cuts him short. "Let it go," he barks. The other man begins to apologize, but Harris goes crazy. "He said let it go!" And Bester realizes the significance—Harris said "he," not "I." He is suffering from a multiple personality disorder.

"Freeze!" Zack cries as Harris and Bryce emerge from their shared quarters. They both pull PPGs, duck down behind some packing cases, and exchange fire. Bester approaches from the other direction, telling Harris he can help. Bryce turns to fire, but Zack shoots, hitting

him in the arm and knocking the PPG from his hand.
Security guards move in to find Harris curled up on the
floor like a frightened child, displaying the fourth of his
personalities.

Bester and Lauren head home with Harris and Bryce
sedated in the back. "We still have the mundane to deal
with," Bester comments, and Lauren asks if she can be
the one to do it. Bester agrees and moments later Bryce's
body tumbles out of their craft, spinning endlessly in the
shifting patterns of hyperspace.

In the fifth year, the story was allowed to take a breather every now and then to explore things there simply hadn't been time for before, particularly in the highly driven fourth season. "The Corps Is Mother, the Corps Is Father" takes the opportunity to look a little closer at Bester and the Psi Corps.

"It was very interesting," says Walter Koenig, who got the lion's share of the episode as Bester. "There were some parts that were terrific from an actor's point of view. I had a scene where he rejected the advances of a young woman, I thought that was a great scene. It showed that he is a very human guy and I think people can relate to that. There will be some guys out there who will say, 'Jerk! why don't you just say "yeah"?' But on the other hand, it shows a very deep, abiding love and loyalty for this woman Carolyn, and he could not in conscience break his vow that he would wait for her. Then there were scenes that were expository, things that had to be included to have a better idea of where the Psi Corps was coming from, and they were not inspiring. They were necessary, but they were not inspiring."

The issue of Bester's inner humanity and his love for Carolyn is something that has been explored before, but not alongside his more sinister side. When Bester first arrived on the station, he was clearly the villain, and as he continued to return, the more subtle parts of his character were revealed. In "The Corps Is Mother, the Corps Is Father," we see both sides of him. This is a man who has committed atrocities, who thinks little of killing "mundanes," but who has a philosophy and a reasoning behind what he does, stemming from a genuine concern for his own people. He thinks telepaths are superior to normals and will follow whatever path he has to, to advance their cause.

"Bester is not a nice guy," writer and executive producer Joe Straczynski explains, "but not everyone sees him in that light, which is why I did one episode from inside the Psi Corps this season, to show how others in the P.C. see him."

Indeed, the two interns who accompany Bester in this episode regard him as a hero. It is not a view that Sheridan or the others would share, but what this episode does is show how someone could take that view, even if it would be unpalatable to most. "What's so marvelous about what Joe has done is he hasn't written the guys in the black hats, the guys in the white hats, he's written complicated characters," actor Walter Koenig says. "God knows I hate to draw this as a comparison because if there was anybody in history in my lifetime who was a total abomination it was Adolf Hitler, but, you know, Adolf Hitler loved dogs. It's easy to understand people if you throw them into a black light and you pitch them in evil terms, you say, 'Ah, that's a bad guy.' It becomes far more complicated if he is the bad guy with a point of view and a sense of values and a motivation that he can justify. If you go all the way back to *Star Trek II* [in which Walter co-starred as Chekov], what made that picture so successful was Khan was a marvelous villain. You felt for this guy, as much as booed him—his wife had died and he wanted vengeance and he loved her. These are the most interesting characters; even though they are bad guys, you can identify with them."

So does he identify with Bester? "I have to. How can I play him if I don't? Within us all is all of the genetic history of mankind, which is aggressive and full of violence. That's what we're a composite of, but we've learned through the process of socialization to inhibit that—but it's there, and the wonderful thing that is available to an actor is the license to search for that and to express it. So whatever his hostility is, whatever the cold merciless part of him is, it's still not something that I imitate, but it is something that I draw upon from my own personality."

The contrasting attitudes to Bester are shown nowhere better than when he leaves the comfortable surroundings of Psi Corps HQ where he is liked and respected, where people call him by his first name, and comes to Babylon 5 where he is sneered at. Zack greets him by asking if he hasn't caused enough trouble for one lifetime, a typical example of the easy banter they share, ridiculing each other without actually resorting to confrontation. The two characters have a wonderful relationship, and it is one reflected on set with the two actors. "Walter's great," Jeff Conaway, who plays Zack, says. "He's a very nice guy, he's very professional, he's good on the set, he jokes. There was one scene . . ." Jeff creases up laughing at the memory. "There was one scene we were doing and we were kind of in the background and then we have some lines. So as we're standing there we're supposed to be talking, and I said to him, 'Look, I've got to go to the bathroom, do you want to wipe me?' He died! *He died!* He turned all sorts of colors of purple, he couldn't get enough of that one! I don't know what prompted me to say that. So that's the kind of friendship we have—I ask him to wipe me!"

"I get along famously with everybody, I don't think there are any exceptions," Walter says. "I had one very brief moment with Andrea Thompson in, I think it was the second season, but other than that everyone's been great. And they treat me so well, they treat me as if I am a member of the family and that makes it very special."

The episode was directed by Stephen Furst, the third time the actor who usually plays Vir was allowed to sit in *Babylon 5*'s director's chair. One scene that "took a while to figure out how to do" was when Bester stares at his reflection in the mirror, trying to put his mind into the position of Harris, the killer, to such an extent that his reflection becomes Harris'. "It's a trick," Stephen reveals. "The trick was he's looking in a mirror and when the camera goes round, the other guy comes in. Then when we come back, the mirror's tilted slightly but the camera can't tell that the mirror's tilted, and we have the reflection of the other guy. So it looks like Walter is looking into the mirror and he sees the reflection of the black guy, but it's really the black guy just standing there next to Walter." The character Jonathan Harris, incidentally, is named after a *Babylon 5* fan who won a raffle at the World Science Fiction Convention in San Antonio in 1997. The prize was to have a character in the show named after you. When he entered, the real Jonathan Harris probably didn't realize his namesake would turn out to be a murderous psychopath.

By the end of the episode, part of the audience might have been ready to concede that maybe Bester is not such a bad guy after all. He cares enough not to take advantage of a young woman in his care, even though she offers herself to him; he tracks down a killer with efficiency and even offers to help the killer overcome his mental illness. But then, at the last, we see the sinister side of his nature return as he "deals with the mundane" by allowing Lauren to throw him out of an air lock to die in hyperspace. "I think his conscience is pretty much free," Walter Koenig concludes. "I think occasionally there are pangs, but I don't think he thinks of himself as sinister. I think he thinks of how he must deal with these people and what he must do to keep them on a level playing field. There's certainly significant evidence that there are people that would like to destroy all telepaths or to render them impotent or take away their powers, so he has to do what he has to do. We see behavior in a police force or in an army in the circumstances of war which is totally justified, but if you see that kind of behavior in civilian life, you would be aghast, and I think that's what we have here."

14
"Meditations on the Abyss"

Cast
President John Sheridan ....Bruce Boxleitner
Michael Garibaldi ....Jerry Doyle
Delenn ....Mira Furlan
Dr. Stephen Franklin ....Richard Biggs
Lennier ....Bill Mumy
Vir Cotto ....Stephen Furst
Zack Allan ....Jeff Conaway
Londo Mollari ....Peter Jurasik
G'Kar ....Andreas Katsulas

Guest Stars
Drazi Ambassador ....Ron Campbell
Findell ....Martin East
Montoya ....Richard Yniguez
Drazi Vendor ....Carl Ciarfalio
Tough Guy ....Vincent Deadrick Jr.
Narn Seeker ....Mark Hendrickson

Delenn slips out of bed and secretly makes her way to Down Below where she has arranged to meet Lennier. She has a mission for him and she does not want Sheridan to know, lest he object to putting a friend in danger. The Alliance needs proof that it is the Centauri who are behind the recent attacks on shipping lanes; she wants Lennier to patrol the Centauri border looking for anything suspicious, under cover as a Ranger trainee on board White Star 27, *commanded by Captain Montoya.*

Vir staggers into Londo's quarters with an armful of parcels. He unpacks, talking about his newfound vice of eating junk food until Londo puts up a hand to silence him. A device in Londo's quarters is beeping. He scans the room with it until the beeps get louder in the direction of one of Vir's parcels. Londo pulls out a listening device that had been planted there and crushes it under his foot. Londo says the bug was planted because of politics, something that Vir will have to learn about. "Yes, Vir," he said. "I have decided that when I am gone, the new ambassador to Babylon 5 will be you!"

One of Lennier's fellow Rangers on the White Star is Findell. In a test where Montoya leaves them stranded in space with a limited amount of air, he is so nervous of failure that he is unable to calm himself into a meditative state to conserve oxygen. Afterwards, Findell tells Lennier he joined the Anla'shok because he felt obliged to carry on the work of his family, who died fighting the Shadow War. "If you're doing this because you feel you should be doing this, not because you want to do it, your purpose is flawed," Lennier tells him.

Vir confronts the Drazi fruit seller who hid the bugging device in one of his parcels, but the vendor dismisses the weak and foolish ambassador's aide, telling him to go away. Vir's expression darkens and he turns away, but only to return with one of Londo's swords. He crashes through the fruit stand waving the blade furiously, with Londo watching proudly from a distance. "Now he is ready to be ambassador for the Centauri," he says.

Montoya sends Lennier and Findell out in the fighters again, this time to pick out thirty-nine homing beacons from an asteroid field. The fighters duck and swoop around the asteroids, firing at the occasional rock that gets in their way. But Findell collects none of the homing beacons; instead, he sets his fighter on a collision course. Lennier targets Findell's engines and fires as the ship is about to ram the asteroid, but it still keeps going. Lennier picks up speed, moves alongside Findell's ship, and whacks it out of the way. But when he looks up, he realizes the asteroid is now heading straight for him. He fires his engines and moves out of the way just in time for the asteroid to graze past him.

Captain Montoya reproaches Lennier for his actions and gives him a fail mark for the exercise. As for Findell, he arranges a special assignment for him, to be stationed on Minbar where he will vet new Anla'shok recruits. "I want you to ask them, from the very bottom of their soul, if this is really what they want to do," he says. It is obvious that Montoya knows exactly what has gone on between the two of them. And later, when Montoya gives Lennier a Centauri message to decode, it is obvious he knew about his secret mission, too.

There was some virus that really had it in for *Babylon 5* during the making of the fifth season. After Robin Atkin Downes had struggled through "In the Kingdom of the Blind" with a nasty flu, it returned to get Bill Mumy. "I had this terrible flu that was going around," Bill, who plays Lennier, remembers. "My family traded it back and forth for six or seven weeks, it was really bad. Unfortunately it happened to fall within a period of a couple of very big Lennier shows, so I'm sure when those shows air everyone will go, 'Wow, listen to him,' because I sound completely different than normal, just completely congested. I was working with 102-degree fever; it was tough.

"I was sad because I had gotten the flu early and I had really done my best to stay home and beat it and to take the antibiotics and rest and everything else," he says. "Then I had this terrible relapse. I was only doing eight episodes of these twenty-two—they're all pretty big Lennier shows—so it was a shame that during these two back to back I had to be ill when we made them. But a lot of people on the crew were ill as well, and that's just part of showbiz sometimes."

The episode begins with Delenn secretly meeting Lennier in Down Below. "I was very sick for that," Bill remembers, "but there's a wonderful, wonderful dark cramped little scene, it's like a three-page scene with Delenn and Lennier in this Down Below quarters after a fight. Lennier, when he kicks ass, is like the Green Hornet or Kato or something. So Lennier kicks ass and saves Delenn from some trouble in Down Below, and then the two of them have this three-page scene together in this little tiny small area, like this little tiny cubicle. It was very dark and shadowy and a very quiet whispering three pages that I recall as being really, really good. I haven't seen it, but, again, working with Mira is always a treat, and the two of us seem to really have a really nice chemistry together. When I see it, optimistically, I'll have the same feeling—of course, I had a fever, so who knows? But when we did it, I thought it was a really powerful scene."

"That was actually the most interesting thing for me to play with that whole story line," Delenn actress Mira Furlan says. "That had the most drama this season. I thought it had some good moments."

There are undercurrents shifting through this scene as we see the faint hope in Lennier that perhaps there is a romantic reason behind Delenn's request to meet him in secret. When he realizes she has called him there to take on a covert mission, his hope fades and he stiffens back into his Ranger persona. What we are left with is the question of why she met him in secret, keeping it from Sheridan, her husband and the president of the Alliance. We later discover it is because he would not have approved of Delenn assigning a possible suicide mission to a close friend. "That's another thing I have a problem with," Mira says. "Delenn, although feeling love and appreciation and a real bond with Lennier, sends him off to a place where he could die, for political reasons. It's hard. Nothing justifies anyone's death, I don't think. I don't believe in big pictures, I privately don't believe in any political reason to die except for, maybe, political freedom."

The relationship between these two characters is perhaps all the stronger because of the friendship between the two actors. *Babylon 5* was Mira's first job after leaving the former Yugoslavia for America, and Billy was the person she came to work with the most. "I feel about Billy as if he's my brother," she says, "my brother from the other side of the world. We have a lot of common traits. We are so different, we come from totally different cultures. I grew up in Zagreb; he grew up in Hollywood. He was in the industry since he was born; I became an actor when I went to study at the academy for theater. I did so much theater, I did the classics, I played at the Croatian national theater, and so on. Billy is a big comic book admirer; my mother is a librarian, and she never allowed me as a child to read comics because it was considered bad for my spiritual development. So we are completely different, really completely, like the opposite. On the other hand we share so many things. We are only children, both of us. These are bad traits, there is this feeling that we are the center of the universe and there is a self-centeredness that has to be controlled, and we always discuss that. I think we can help each other in many ways, we can understand each other, and actually, I see him with all his faults and he sees me with all my faults because we share them in some weird sense. It's so strange and actually so moving, so great, to find somebody like that who grew up in totally different circumstances, but who shares so much with you."

When Lennier boards the White Star and undertakes his mission, we see why Delenn had so much faith in him, in his noble and self-sacrificing efforts to save the young Findell. The episode makes the point that if you are going to do something, you should do it because you want to, not because you feel you should. It relates back to earlier in the season when the Minbari Ranger tutor, Turval, discussed Marcus' death with Delenn. He said it was not unexpected because Marcus joined the Rangers for the wrong reasons, to atone for the death of his brother, the same reason that Findell became a Ranger.

The change brought about for G'Kar in this episode is, on the surface, a cosmetic one as, at last, he gets his second red eye back, thanks to a new alien implant that replaces the old Human blue one. Before this, actor Andreas Katsulas hadn't been wearing only one contact lens, as you might expect, but two. His own eyes are brown, so he wore one blue lens and one red lens. The change, therefore, didn't make any physical difference to him, but he feels it was good for G'Kar. "I like it more," he says. "I think the character has more of a mystery to him when both his eyes are red. There's something unsettling about those two different-colored eyes. I can't quite put my finger on it. It's too much of an intellectual idea, it does not ring true somehow. I prefer to see them both blue, or both brown, or both red."

We see that G'Kar, who had returned from Centauri Prime as a religious icon, has been giving talks to his fellow Narns on the station, even though he admits to Franklin that he is rather confused about the whole thing. During this particular gathering, he is asked a question about truth and God, and he replies with a wonderful speech. Andreas is one of the most praised actors working on the show, but he takes a modest line when it comes to delivering speeches. "These actors and this ensemble, with being dressed as G'Kar and in the makeup I think I can get away with it," he says. "But if you put me in another set of circumstances and got me to play this character, I would just be very heavy-handed in my way of making a speech.

"Actually, when I worked for [acclaimed theater director] Peter Brook for all those years, he gave speeches like that to people who could really do them well. So I never got to say nice things, I was always the low comic relief. That was my forte, sort of broad farce, and I got used a lot like that. Sometimes I also played some very black characters, but I'm not really gifted with speechmaking. Peter [Jurasik] is very good at it and some of the others can handle it, but I said to Joe, 'Give me good lines and not a lot of them,' and he actually did that, he gave me some really choice lines and I didn't have to speak for pages."

Whatever G'Kar's skill in making the speech to the assembled Narns, it falls on deaf ears. They are only appeased when he answers their questions with bland statements like "Truth is a river." So much for profundity. Although G'Kar has touched a lot of people with his Book of G'Kar, not everyone is prepared to see the philosophy behind it, preferring a religion based on catch phrases and idolatry. In that light, it is easy to understand why G'Kar feels he has to escape later on in the season.

15
"Darkness Ascending"

Cast

President John Sheridan	Bruce Boxleitner
Michael Garibaldi	Jerry Doyle
Delenn	Mira Furlan
Dr. Stephen Franklin	Richard Biggs
Lennier	Bill Mumy
Vir Cotto	Stephen Furst
Zack Allan	Jeff Conaway
Lyta Alexander	Patricia Tallman
Londo Mollari	Peter Jurasik
G'Kar	Andreas Katsulas

Guest Stars

Shadow (Garibaldi)	Jerry Doyle
Lyse Hampton-Edgars	Denise Gentile
Minister	Thomas MacGreevy
Maitre D'	Wesley Mask
Businessman	Edmund Shaff
Montoya	Richard Yniguez

Garibaldi, bloodied and battered, staggers into the Zocalo. Death and carnage are all around him. Sheridan's body lies slumped against the wall where, above his head, someone has scrawled "you failed me." Garibaldi moves on past the bodies and turns when he hears someone call his name. It is Franklin, bleeding and unable to pull himself to his feet. "We needed you," he begins, but a shot fires through the gloom and strikes Franklin dead. Garibaldi hears laughter and looks through the ruddy haze to see that the perpetrator of all this death and destruction is himself.

Garibaldi bolts awake with a yell. Then he sees Lyta, sitting at the end of his bed, her eyes glowing Vorlon-white. "You shouldn't have woken up, this was just a dream. This never happened," she says. There's a flash of white and Garibaldi sits up in bed with a yell, sweating, panting, scared, uncertain what is real and what is not. Then his door opens and he grabs his PPG, pointing at the female silhouette in the doorway. It is Lise. "Is that any way to welcome the love of your life, Michael?" she asks.

Sheridan has discovered Delenn's little secret. She sent Lennier off on a dangerous mission without telling him, and Sheridan has recalled the White Star he was serving on. They argue about who should have told what to whom, but that soon becomes academic as the captain of the White Star informs them Lennier is missing in a one-man fighter, with enough air to last only thirty-six hours.

Lyta has tried everywhere to get money and transport for rogue telepaths and has ended up at G'Kar's door, prepared to consider the very offer she refused when she first arrived on Babylon 5. He can have her telepath DNA—and that of hundreds of others if he wants it—to help breed Narn telepaths, as long as he gives her the means to help her own people in return.

Lennier, barely conscious, with his air almost spent, stirs to the sound of an alarm from his ship. He is approaching a Centauri war cruiser, one that he hopes will confirm the Centauri are behind the recent attacks. He guides his ship alongside and extends claws that attach themselves to the hull and a hose that burrows inside and draws out fresh oxygen with a satisfying hiss. A jump point forms ahead of them and the cruiser carries Lennier's small fighter right to its base of operations.

Lennier is carried along to the cruiser's next target, emerging into normal space where the cruiser fires on several transport ships. One of the pilots screams over the communications channel, "We surrender, we surrender . . ." but the Centauri war cruiser fires its guns regardless, slicing the other ships mercilessly into pieces. Lennier witnesses it all and, when the carnage is over, detaches from the cruiser and floats away with the debris.

Delenn is so overcome when she hears Lennier is safe that she hugs Londo. But her celebrations are marred by the sense of foreboding that falls over the station. The information Lennier risked his life to obtain means the Alliance is about to face its first big test.

As soon as Garibaldi hears the news, he rushes back to his quarters where he tells Lise to leave the station immediately. "Barring an act of God," he tells her, "by this time tomorrow, we're going to be at war with the Centauri."

Darkness ascends on all the characters in this episode as events conspire to bring them down, threatening the lives of individuals and the fragile peace held together by the Alliance. It begins with Garibaldi's foreboding dream, a stark series of images that suggest disaster is coming to the station and Garibaldi will be the one to allow it to happen.

It was the highlight of the episode for Janet Greek, who, as director, really got the chance to do something visually interesting with the sequence. "I did a lot of handheld camera movement, I moved the camera a lot, I did a lot of Dutch angles—Dutch angles are like off angles. We had two camera operators and I had them moving the lens constantly, then I just had them intercut all those real oddly so they changed around. It will be interesting to see what that looks like cut together [by the producers] because I cut it in a very MTVish way, very out of sequence. That was a lot of fun, and the art department did a great job on the set of that one, too, made the set look really horrific, the aftermath of a big battle and stuff."

The reason for Garibaldi letting down his friends must be his drinking, which is something he still refuses to acknowledge. Lise returns from Mars and finds that he has turned back to his old ways. "Her poor character," Garibaldi actor Jerry Doyle laments. "She's in love with this guy who's lost his job, he's a drunk, he's a pain in the ass, says I'm going away for two weeks to Babylon 5 to work some stuff out and she doesn't see him for six months, he doesn't call, but she keeps coming back. We talked about making sure there was a point where the character could find some strength instead of just looking like a doormat. So we worked on that and tried to get some things tweaked and I think she pulled it off."

This episode is classic *Babylon 5* fare. It has a main story running through it, as one would expect, and various interweaving elements belonging to other stories, but its main purpose is to set up the conflict with the Centauri. The often-used technique of foreshadowing is used once again in Garibaldi's dream, and the whole episode races toward the inevitable conclusion of war. Highlighted within that is the fate of Londo, a man divorced from the decisionmaking on Centauri Prime, unaware of the destruction wreaked on other races by his people's warships. By the end of the episode, not only has evidence been revealed to implicate the Centauri, but also there is the sense that Londo is being propelled once again down the path of darkness.

The main story of the episode focuses on Lennier's mission, which actor Bill Mumy calls his "James Bond arc." While Garibaldi turns to drink to try and disguise the pain he is feeling over the terrible things he has experienced, Lennier throws himself headlong into a dangerous mission, risking his life to the point of suffocation. "Again, Lennier is willing to get the job done at any cost for the betterment of the whole and certainly for Delenn. It's almost like he doesn't care if he lives or dies, he just wants to get the job done for her," he says.

How interesting it is to compare this Lennier with the Lennier who first came aboard the station with his wide-eyed innocence. Like G'Kar, who made the transition over five years from warrior to religious icon, Lennier has turned from the devout—perhaps naïve—graduate of a Minbari temple to a Ranger prepared to put his life on the line. "Well, yes and no," Bill says. "Because actually he's still a very religious person. I don't think Lennier was necessarily naïve, I think if you go back and look at him he was extremely inquisitive and open to all of this new stuff around him. I think the Shadow War hardened him a bit to that stuff. I mean, here's a guy who was a priest in a temple and then working for someone he not only admires because of her position on the Grey Council, but he then grows to become deeply in love with, in an unrequited way, and then he finds himself as communications and weapons officer on the number-one battleship in this great war. So yes, he has had a big arc. I suppose I shouldn't say he wasn't naïve, but I don't think he was ever unprepared. I think Lennier has always been capable and very selfless."

Lennier's mission brings out a certain tension between Sheridan and Delenn. The way Delenn sneaked out of their quarters to ask Lennier to do this dangerous job for her, deliberately concealing it from Sheridan, and the way Sheridan, when he found out, recalled the White Star without consulting her is a matter of contention. For Joe Straczynski, this was just the type of tension he wanted to exploit in the fifth year. "For any couple when they're first married, that first year is difficult at best," he says. "Trying to balance that with the reality of running an empire, and the strains that come with that, pulls them in various directions. It's given us different kinds of conflict to play with."

But the matter is soon resolved and the pair have to admit they were wrong to try to maintain secrets from each other. There is no getting away from the fact that these two people are right for each other and marriage suits them very well.

Bruce Boxleitner agrees. "I'm the president and that has certain restraints," he says. He decided the best way to take the relationship was to enrich the feeling of the two of them as an established couple. "Mira and Bruce have finally realized we had better make this much more physical on screen, much warmer, and feel like two married people. I think the way it's been written, we're going on setting the future with our child and it's going on to this logical thing. I think the relationship is very, very full this year. I don't know what else we could do—we got married."

Within the big story of the Centauri's actions, and the consequences leading from that, is Lyta's personal struggle to build a new life for telepaths. We see her trying and failing to get a commercial agreement with the business community and having to resort to G'Kar, the person she initially turned away from in the pilot. "We kind of just picked up right where we left off," actress Patricia Tallman says. "I don't know how it's all edited together, but Lyta goes in there—at least in mind—fully prepared that if G'Kar says, 'Okay, I'll take the deal, but it has to be a physical mating,' in other words, 'You have to have sex with me,' then she would go, 'Okay.' At this point she'll do anything. She's tried everything to get the equipment she needs to start pushing the telepaths in the direction she needs to go. He's the last shot she has. I hope you see that in my performance."

Since their first scene in the pilot, G'Kar and Lyta really haven't had many dealings with each other. In fact, this is only the second scene Pat and Andreas Katsulas have had with just the two of them. "He's adorable, he's wonderful," Pat says of her fellow actor. "He's very generous and giving. I mean, he's very self-deprecating. Sometimes you work with actors who are as experienced as Andreas and Peter, and they will be a little pompous or direct you or make suggestions. He never does. He's so generous, he's like, 'No, no, no, you know what you're doing, you're wonderful, go for it.' I'm very comfortable working with him, we have a lot of fun. I'm just really glad that that's a question that gets answered because it's been hanging around for five years."

16
"And All My Dreams, Torn Asunder"

Cast
President John Sheridan ....Bruce Boxleitner
Michael Garibaldi ....Jerry Doyle
Delenn ....Mira Furlan
Dr. Stephen Franklin ....Richard Biggs
Lennier ....Bill Mumy
Vir Cotto ....Stephen Furst
Zack Allan ....Jeff Conaway
Londo Mollari ....Peter Jurasik
G'Kar ....Andreas Katsulas

Guest Stars
Minister.......................................Thomas MacGreevy
Drazi Ambassador ....Kim Strauss
Brakiri Ambassador ....Jonathan Chapman
Brakiri ....Vincent Deadrick Jr.

Sheridan follows the flickering candlelight into the main room of Delenn's quarters, where she sits staring at the flame. "You should sleep. It'll be morning soon," he says gently. "You'll need all your strength for what's ahead." She nods, but doesn't move, just continues to contemplate the burning candle.

Londo is shut out of the Alliance meeting where evidence that the Centauri are behind the attacks on shipping lanes is being presented. The response is a vote to blockade. Londo reports this to the regent back on Centauri Prime and is told by the minister that "He pronounced it the most clever fraud he has ever seen." Londo doesn't believe Sheridan and the others can be lying, but he wants to believe even more that his people have nothing to do with the attacks.

Londo faces the Alliance on behalf of his government

*and announces they are leaving the Alliance and defying
the legality of the blockade. "From now on," he tells
them, "all Centauri transports entering Alliance space
will be accompanied by our finest warships. Anyone
who fires on our ships will be committing an act of
war."*

Garibaldi stands, a little unsteady on his feet, and
opens the door to Zack, who has been sent to find him.
Garibaldi snaps about falling asleep, but there is
something in his manner that catches Zack's eye. Zack
picks up an orange from the fruit bowl on the table and
throws it at him. Garibaldi misses. He's drunk and no
matter how much he protests, nothing will change that
fact. "If you report me, they'll drop kick me and I can
kiss my career good-bye," Garibaldi implores. "Just give
me a little time, okay?" Zack softens and agrees to help
him get into shape for his meeting with Sheridan.

Sheridan asks Garibaldi to coordinate reports from
Rangers who are watching the Centauri warships and
the Alliance worlds who have stationed their own
cruisers ready to fire if the Centauri violate their space. If
the White Stars can get there before fighting starts,
maybe they can avert a war.

But when the vital message comes through to
Garibaldi, he is asleep in a drunken stupor. The
jumpgate in the Drazi system crackles open and
Centauri warships stream out. A Drazi squadron moves
to block the way, the Centauri return fire, and space
becomes awash with explosions and energy blasts.

Ambassadors charge into the Alliance chambers,
furious that Sheridan broke his promise to protect them
with the White Star fleet. Their cacophony of voices gets
louder and louder until Sheridan shouts at them to be
quiet. "You want war, is that it?" he demands, searching
their faces. "You want war? You got a war."

The news reaches Londo via the minister on Centauri
Prime, where he has returned with G'Kar as his
bodyguard. In the light of what has happened, the regent
orders that G'Kar be imprisoned. "No," Londo says. "I

told you before; where I go, he goes. And where he goes,
I go." Moments later, he is gazing at the moonlight
filtering in through the tiny window of a cell he is to
share with G'Kar.

Delenn sits in her quarters, gazing into the flickering
flame of a candle. It represents life, she tells Sheridan.
"When it goes out, it is gone forever . . . So many
candles will go out tonight. I wonder that we can see
anything at all, some days."

The effect of Garibaldi's alcoholism has begun to spread
wider. It is not just a friend he gets killed this time, or a
mission he is unable to carry out—this time his drunkenness
helps drag the whole Interstellar Alliance into war.

Jerry Doyle, as it turned out, was able to relate quite
strongly to his character's addiction. "I quit smoking at the
time," he says. "What I would try to do is get the feeling of
wanting a drink. I knew I wanted a cigarette, so when I was
doing a scene about whether I'm going to have a drink or
not, that little good guy on the shoulder, bad guy on the
shoulder kind of thing, it was the same dilemma of wanting a
cigarette as it was of wanting a drink. So mentally I kind of
knew what that was all about."

It was not a stunt he pulled to get closer to Garibaldi, it
was a genuine attempt to give up tobacco. "I wanted to quit
smoking. It didn't work, obviously," Jerry says, puffing on his
cigarette. At least it's marginally better than the giant cigars
he was smoking the year before. "I started chain smoking
cigars, so I figured in order to save money I'd go back to
cigarettes. I quit for like two months, which was kind of the
length the story arc went, then it was like, 'Fuck this, give
me a cigarette!' But I understand the problems and the pressures that the alcoholic goes through and waging that battle,
because for me it was the same thing with cigarettes."

As for playing drunk, he has a few tricks up his sleeve. "If
you try and do it too physically obvious, it almost becomes
slapstick," he says. "What I would do in the scenes where I
had to be really bombed, where I had to get busted or di-
sheveled, right before they said 'action' I would be standing

off camera and I would spin in a circle. Right after they said 'action' I would stop spinning and walk into the room, and when you're trying to walk straight, you're rigid but you always get that one little bump or hiccup in your walk. Then when they came in for the closeups, my eyes were kind of glazed because I'm trying to focus on whoever I'm talking to. I think, in the beginning, if you establish the scene for the audience, then they'll not notice later that you're kind of back to almost you in terms of clarity and diction. Hopefully in the beginning it sells the scene enough so they know what you're trying to do."

"And All My Dreams, Torn Asunder" is the first time Garibaldi appears drunk in front of the people he cares about. This time it is Zack, a friend and a colleague. Out of that friendship comes a trust, and although Zack should have reported Garibaldi before his problem dragged them into a war, his personal loyalty is just that little bit stronger. It is a strong relationship between them—bonded through some incident in the past that is referred to once again here, but not specified—and one that is shared between the two actors. "We get along real well; I like Jerry a lot," Jeff Conaway, who plays Zack, says. "And I like him in the show, I think he's real good in it. When I first started watching the show he was my favorite character, maybe he still is. We joke around, we have a good time. I don't know what it was, but when we first started working together, we talked a lot and we shared our past and we bonded and we became friends. I think that came across, and maybe Joe saw that happening and incorporated it into the script. He's a very interesting, intelligent guy, very funny, very quick-witted, and I think we kind of meshed together well. We're both from New York, we've got that sense, that street sense about us. He's had a different life than I have, but in some ways similar. We've had similar heartbreaks in our past and we were able to kind of commiserate over them."

The war is obviously devastating to the Alliance, but it also has personal consequences for Londo. On one side are the facts presented to him that incriminate his own people in the attacks, while on the other is his desire to believe the evidence is a fraud. Londo is trapped in the middle, blamed for the actions of his government that he does not want to believe are true and forced to deny them on its behalf. "What was wonderful about the structure of the script was, one by one, people bring him the evidence," Peter Jurasik, who plays Londo, says. "So Londo is progressively getting isolated and feeling betrayed by more and more people. He has nowhere to let it out. Poor Vir has to hang around and, we assume, have dinner with him all these nights, but other than that he has nowhere to let his tension out. So Joe, in a very nice way, built up to that moment. It was up to the audience to figure out how he's going to react. But he is, of course, the old Londo—don't turn on the Centauri if you want to stay on his good side. He's a man with complete blinders for politics and his people."

The consequence of that takes him back to Centauri Prime, where he can be at the heart of his government, and once again G'Kar accompanies him as his bodyguard. But when war breaks out, Londo's insistence that he goes wherever the Narn does backfires, and he ends up in a cell with him. "Yeah, it was a fun moment to play," Peter says. "It's great to see any character get caught up in that much self-pride and arrogance as Londo did. But the serious part of the story is that it continues to isolate him. By putting him in prison he's isolated by his own people, he's isolated from Vir, he's just getting more and more isolated. It's just a dangerous position to push Londo into because then he gets wrapped into his own mind, and his wheels start spinning, and he loses more and more contact with what really might be going on."

The episode was directed by Goran Gajic, Mira Furlan's husband, who worked extensively as a director in Yugoslavia and left the country for America with her. His debut on *Babylon 5* came after a long campaign by the producers to let him have a go, as Joe Straczynski explains: "Goran has had a hard time breaking in over here. We showed Warners his showreel, which is very art oriented, and they never really got behind the notion of him doing one for us. Then we showed it to TNT and said, 'Every so often you have to do one for the angels. This is a talented guy, let's give him a chance.' And TNT, to their credit, said we could do it. The nice thing about this position is every once in a while, it gives you a magic wand and you can use it for the betterment of someone else." [*Dreamwatch*, issue 45]

Mira found it a very easy experience to work with her husband, as they had worked together before. "We made a movie together before we left and it's called *Dear Video*, an epistolary comedy where I play this young lady who falls in love through video letters with a German count. It's a comedy, and it's a wacky comedy, and that's what Goran loves to do. So this was a departure from that kind of world of outrageous comedies that he used to do in Yugoslavia, the genre of science fiction. But I think he really enjoyed working here, and I think people enjoyed working with him, and I was very pleased that it happened after five years.

"But, you know, there is a pressure, definitely, especially on this set because I wanted everything to be fine. There's also the pressure of time. Will he be on time? Will the producers come at a certain point and look at their watch? And all these considerations. So that particular situation had its own pressures on both of us, as you can imagine."

The episode, although it is about the start of a war, begins and ends in a very thoughtful mood with Delenn staring into the flame of a candle. She explains to Sheridan in the final scene that the flame represents life. She follows that with a long, delicate speech about the sanctity of life and her fears for how many lives will be lost in the war. Having come from the civil war in Yugoslavia, the speech once again taps into Mira's personal experience. "Absolutely," she says, "so many things do in this show. It's a beautiful speech, and Joe writes these beautiful things. He really thinks and he writes about politics and the whole way this world operates in such a brilliant way. He's such a brilliant man and that's such a rare thing in this world. That's why *Babylon 5* is so interesting for me. That's the biggest quality of this show. There is also the action adventure and shooting and blowing up, which is not why I love this show. It's this other stuff, these thoughts."

17
"Movements of Fire and Shadow"

Cast

President John Sheridan	Bruce Boxleitner
Michael Garibaldi	Jerry Doyle
Delenn	Mira Furlan
Dr. Stephen Franklin	Richard Biggs
Captain Elizabeth Lochley	Tracy Scoggins
Lennier	Bill Mumy
Vir Cotto	Stephen Furst
Lyta Alexander	Patricia Tallman
Londo Mollari	Peter Jurasik
G'Kar	Andreas Katsulas

Guest Stars

Drakh	Wayne Alexander
Kulomani	Josh Clark
Na'Tok	Robin Sachs
Daro	Bart McCarthy
Lt. Corwin	Joshua Cox
Minister #1	Thomas MacGreevy
Dr. Li Terana Varda	Neil Bradley
Regent	Damian London

"We're going to need bigger ships," Sheridan tells
Delenn over breakfast. *He's ordered the White Stars into
the war and they can't keep holding their own against
warships up to six times their size. Delenn agrees to go
to Minbar to ask, in secret, for help in creating a new
class of ship.*

*A bright light flashes through Londo and G'Kar's cell,
and they both fall unconscious. The wall of their cell
slides away and grey, alien hands remove Londo's body.
Londo is laid flat on his back while instruments probe
his body and aliens whisper in another language around*

him. He stirs in frightened semiconsciousness and the eyes of a Drakh peer over him. "Yes, he will be sufficient," it says.

Londo cries out and jerks awake. He is back in the cell. "I have to get out of here," he says in panic. "But I have to do it so that I do not lose face." G'Kar puts his hands together and concentrates until his stomach muscles spew up last night's supper. The disgusting stench is excuse enough.

Garibaldi rushes into Sheridan's quarters and hands him a report. The Drazi and the Narn have decided to attack Centauri Prime.

Franklin and Lyta have arrived on the Drazi Homeworld on a mercy mission from Vir, to find out what's happening to the bodies of the Centauri killed in battle. As they question one of the planet's doctors, two Drazi drop into their hotel room from the balcony above. Franklin dives for cover, pulls out a PPG, and fires, taking one of them out. Lyta concentrates on the other until, with a bewildered face, the Drazi raises his own gun to his head and fires. The Drazi doctor races for the door, but Franklin slams it shut.

The doctor leads Franklin and Lyta to a research center where the interiors of the Centauri warships are being examined. There are no bodies here, just jet-black, egg-shaped objects. Lyta touches one of them and senses the Shadow technology behind it. These are the things controlling the Centauri ships, not people. Most of the Centauri might not even know what their ships have been up to, leading Franklin to speculate that an outside force may have provoked the war in the Centauri's name, to ensure Centauri Prime is attacked.

Delenn's White Star turns sharply as four Centauri warships loom at its tail. They fire without warning, striking the White Star with a volley of blasts, sending it spinning out of control through hyperspace. Inside, a few small lights dimly glow, illuminating a mess of debris and destroyed instruments. Most of the crew are dead, the engines are off-line, and there's little power left. Delenn stirs out of unconsciousness to find Lennier sitting above her. "This is bad, then," she manages. "Very bad, Delenn," he says.

The regent is looking despondently out of his window on Centauri Prime, talking about his impending death. Londo tries to talk him out of his morbid thoughts, but he keeps talking about "they," people who say things to him and tell him to do things. The regent says the last thing "they" told him to do was send away all ships guarding Centauri Prime and turn off the defense network. A sudden terror descends over Londo's face. "No!" he cries, running down the corridor, looking around helplessly for someone or something to stop them. But there is nothing he can do, and running outside onto the steps of the palace, he looks up to see fleets of alien ships swarming above him.

Events tumble toward devastation in "Movements of Fire and Shadow" with a momentum almost of their own. No one who is caught up in the game really understands the whole picture. They only see part of it, reacting in ways that they feel are right without fully understanding the consequences of their actions. The Drazi want to strike at Centauri Prime in retribution for attacks on their ships, but they cannot know that it is not the Centauri who are ultimately responsible for the war. Not even the Centauri regent, who is giving the orders for the attacks, understands what is going on. Only perhaps at the end, when he is looking out of the window, waiting for the bombs to drop, does he seem to grasp the implications with any kind of clarity.

All these events have been orchestrated from behind the throne. The keeper, first glimpsed on the neck of the regent during Season Four's "Epiphanies," is now controlling him, and he is forced to obey the instructions of its masters, the Drakh. Their manipulation of events is so carefully planned that it would be beautiful if it were not so tragic. Everyone is the loser in this war—transport ships and their crews are destroyed, the fragile peace that held the Alliance together is shattered, and by the end of the episode, Centauri Prime is destined to be devastated. This is the planet's fate that was first glimpsed in the flash forward in Season Three's "War without End." There, a much older Londo presided over his ruined Homeworld with a keeper at his neck. We can see the wheels of destiny turning in "Movements of Fire and Shadow," not only with the impending attack on Centauri Prime, but also with Londo's temporary abduction by aliens who size him up to be the keeper's next host.

"It was great stuff," Peter Jurasik, who plays Londo, remembers. "John Flinn [usually Babylon 5's man behind the camera] was directing, and, of course he had a ball. It was probably the closest Babylon 5 will ever get to an X-Files episode. The aliens were the kind of traditional aliens that you see on every sci-fi show—big-eyed, long-fingered, probing people—and I thought it was a wonderful way to play it. It was fun and John had a ball shooting it, he really did. I remember with that one specific scene, he took a whole morning to shoot it. It put us in the dumper for the rest of the day, but hopefully it will be worthwhile."

After that experience, Londo wakes up back in the cell with G'Kar. If some of the events of the past can be said to have been designed to push these two disparate characters together, then this was the ultimate—locking them in a cell together. "This was a moment that when Joe wrote it we thought, no, he's goofing on us," Peter remembers. "He doesn't really want us to do that?"

But sticking them together in such an unlikely situation produces some of the classic banter that has become the nature of the Londo/G'Kar relationship. It is almost a comic routine with two people who, on the surface, hate each other, but underneath share a friendship. "Oh yeah, absolutely," Peter says. "They're well beyond friendship, they're starting to mirror each other and see themselves in each other. Yeah, they are friends, but they're even more than that to each other. [It's an interesting] relationship of a bodyguard and him protecting Londo and him trying to teach Londo about the light and the spiritual side, being able to provide him with reflections of the darkness that he's in. These two characters, they really are joined at the hip, and for that reason, Joe can take them anywhere he wants. Comedy just becomes a simple entree to slide over. They are a little comedy team; they are the Odd Couple."

Being trapped in a cell with G'Kar cannot, in the end, help the Centauri. After waking from the "nightmare" of being probed for the Drakh, Londo needs to get out. Finding an excuse that will get him out without losing face is up to G'Kar, who obliges by discharging certain intestinal, highly volatile gases. Fortunately, it was a sight the audience was spared by having it happen off-camera. "The moment when he's leaving the cell and talking back to the guard about how vile it all was, those are great moments to play," Peter says. "I get to really play it out, release it all. It's not that intellectual, stuck-in-his-head, studied Londo, the Londo who's trying to figure out everything, all the angst and pain and sadness and pathos that surrounds this character—it's just fun stuff to play. Andreas and I just had a fun time together. That's when we always think we should go on a vaudeville tour together, the 'Londo and G'Kar tour.' "

Elsewhere, the investigations continue into some of the puzzling facts behind the attacks by the Centauri. Ostensibly on a mercy mission for Vir, Franklin and Lyta travel to the Drazi Homeworld. It is here that we first see the hard, tough Lyta that has emerged from the tragedy of Byron's death. She demands a fee for the job so large that it makes Vir flop down in a chair. Then she uses her powers to make a Drazi shoot himself in the head.

The trip to Drazi may have been a hard, no-nonsense business venture for Lyta, but for the actress who plays her, it was just an enjoyable day working with Richard Biggs on Drazi. "I think he's my favorite," Pat Tallman says. "Probably because I've had more scenes with him. We have fun. I'll go to his house and rehearse. I take my kid over there with me and we set him up with a basketball game or something, and then he and I just play with it and we have the best time.

"So we have a scene where it's just an exposition scene, it's a scene that establishes Franklin and Lyta on Drazi, and we're looking at a map and it's a very complicated map, it looks like a child's origami game and it all folds in these weird ways. Rick's being a typical guy—I mean, Franklin is. So we just started improvising, he's looking at the map and going, 'Here we are, it's this way,' and I said, 'You don't really know where you're going, do you? You're just making this up!' Meanwhile aliens are bumping into us and I'm like, 'Weirdo! Look at this place, it stinks!' And he's going, 'Will you calm down?' and it was just so funny! I said men never ask for directions—what is that? What *is* that?! Flinn was having a great time, he was our director. It was a fun day, it felt like a no-pressure day for some reason, we got everything we needed to get. I love working on sets like that, too. Drazi's very atmospheric, and I was having an argument with one of the extras who had a bunch of textured fabrics, tapestry-type fabrics, and he's acting like he's selling these tapestry fabrics. I come up to him and go, 'These aren't from Drazi,' and he said, 'What do you mean?' 'These are from Mexico or somewhere, these aren't from Drazi, you're a charlatan, aren't you?' He's going, 'No, no, lady, these are from Drazi. Cheap, cheap. Fifteen dollars.' It was just one of those great days.

"It was my last time working with Rick Biggs, and we were very aware of that," she continues. "That was actually more sad than my actual last day, I think. I had a couple of moments on my last day like when the crew applauded me and where I just thought I was going to die. I thought, oh shoot, I'm losing it. I was actually okay for a moment there, and I was walking away, and I turned and saw one of our crew members who saw me and waved good-bye and that was more poignant and more sad. It was weird and I almost lost it."

What Lyta and Franklin find on Drazi is evidence that the Centauri are not necessarily the ones behind the war. Yes, they are using Centauri ships, but because they are controlled remotely, it is likely very few people in the Centauri military know about the attacks. It is valuable information in tackling the conflict that threatens to break the Alliance apart, but it comes too late to save Centauri Prime.

18
"The Fall of Centauri Prime"

Cast

President John Sheridan ....Bruce Boxleitner
Michael Garibaldi ....Jerry Doyle
Delenn ....Mira Furlan
Dr. Stephen Franklin ....Richard Biggs
Lennier ....Bill Mumy
Vir Cotto ....Stephen Furst
Zack Allan ....Jeff Conaway
Londo Mollari ....Peter Jurasik
G'Kar ....Andreas Katsulas

Guest Stars

Regent ....Damian London
Drakh ....Wayne Alexander
Na'Tok ....Robin Sachs
Ranger ....Simon Billig
Morden ....Ed Wasser
Adira Tyree ....Fabiana Udenio

Energy weapons light up the night sky as Narn and Drazi ships fire down on Centauri Prime, shaking the planet surface with a myriad of explosions. Londo bangs on G'Kar's cell door, pushing it open against the rubble inside to get to G'Kar's barely conscious body. He manages to pull him out seconds before another explosion rocks the building and the ceiling collapses.

A Drakh emerges from behind the regent to face Londo. "You are now what we need you to be," it tells him. "A beaten, resentful people . . . who can be used . . . Perfect ground for us to do our work. Quietly, quietly . . ." Londo approaches the Drakh unafraid, but stops when he sees the trigger in its hand, capable of setting off a multitude of fusion bombs planted across the planet. The only way to save millions of Centauri lives is to give the Drakh what they want. "What we want from you," the creature tells Londo, "is you."

Lennier sits on the floor next to Delenn in their crippled White Star, their life support running out and their navigational thrusters due to fail and cast them adrift in hyperspace. "I'm sorry, Delenn," he says.

"You risked your life to save me," G'Kar says to Londo as he walks into the room. But Londo is in a somber mood; he has come to say good-bye. Somehow, for reasons even he doesn't understand, it seems important to him. "Isn't it strange, G'Kar," he reflects, "when you and I first met, I had no power and all the choices I could ever want. Now I have all the power I could ever want and no choices at all." He moves to leave, but G'Kar calls him back. He tells Londo that his people can never forgive the Centauri for what they have done to the Narn, "but I can forgive you." And Londo is suddenly touched—deeply and unexpectedly. He puts his hand gently on G'Kar's arm for a moment, then turns away, to face what he must face.

Londo stands before the Drakh and takes off his jacket. "I'm ready," he says. The Drakh opens its robe to reveal a creature, pulsating with life, on its chest. The keeper separates from its host and drops to the floor. It scuttles over to Londo and begins the climb up his leg. Londo doesn't flinch, he just stares ahead expressionless as a tendril reaches up behind him and stabs into his shoulder.

Londo contacts Sheridan at the White Star fleet around Centauri Prime to inform him the Centauri warships are being recalled. He blames the attacks on the late, mad regent, and they agree to end hostilities. Sheridan has just one personal favor to ask—that Londo help find Delenn's missing White Star.

Delenn's White Star beeps a proximity warning as a Centauri warship heads in their direction. With their power depleted, they have no hope of defending themselves. The beeping gets louder, faster, becoming an

almost continuous tone. It is the sound of impending
death, and in those last moments, Lennier turns to
Delenn and says softly, "I love you." But the beeping
stops, suddenly. The Centauri warship has come to save
them, not kill them.

The giant holographic image of Londo in his new
emperor's coat towers above the devastated Centauri
capital. "We fought alone and we will rebuild alone,"
says his defiant voice, echoing across the globe. "We will
work even harder to show those who have come to
humiliate us that we will not bow down."

Londo dismisses Sheridan, Delenn, Vir, and G'Kar
from his world, and as temple bells ring out for every
Centauri life that has been lost, he walks to his
emperor's inauguration, totally alone.

The depth of emotion in "The Fall of Centauri Prime" is
the most intense of Season Five. So much had been
building to this moment; the personal and political maneuverings that had been set in motion early on begin to culmi-
nate in this episode. This was precisely what Joe Straczynski
was alluding to when some viewers complained in the first
half of the season that the stories didn't have the impact
they were expecting. "This was what I wanted to do with the
fifth season," the writer says. "Once again, it has to do with
process and change and how one new set of events rises out
of the ashes of the last one . . . The remaining episodes of
this season represent some of the very best work we've
ever done, maybe even the best work we've done, but they
wouldn't have *nearly* the impact they will have if we hadn't
done what was done in the first half of this season." [on the
Internet]

The events of the earlier episodes have been building
toward the attack on Centauri Prime and the battles in
space. Although devastating in themselves, the emotion and
the drama do not lie in bombs falling on a planet or ships hit
by energy weapons, but in how the characters are affected.
For Delenn and Lennier, the damage suffered by their ship is
a terrible thing, but it is what they are experiencing in what

could be their last moment alive together that elicits the drama. Lennier, sitting with a broken leg in a crippled White Star with, he believes, death imminent, says the three words that he will not get another chance to say: "I love you."

"I think that that scene had already been said," Lennier actor Bill Mumy says. "I think Lennier and Delenn had that moment in a much more articulate exchange when he left to join the Rangers. It wasn't a mystery—he said to her, 'I'm not comfortable here and it's not his fault and it's not your fault, but . . .' and she says, 'I know how you feel.' They wanted me to play that I was shattered that I had said that— and I did. I believed it when we did that, I believed that I was shattered for having said that. Delenn does love Lennier, I wanted her to respond 'I love you too,' and I think she should have. It's not a matter of sex. I mean, certainly Lennier desires her as a woman, but he does have a pure love for her. He's been very noble with his love, and I think, how can she not love him? Love him like you love your German shepherd, love him like you love your best friend, love him like you love your brother or whatever, but she certainly has a love for Lennier. There have been moments in certain episodes where you see Delenn could have gone another way, she could have had a physical relationship with Lennier. I wish they had, that would have made the betrayal [in "Objects at Rest"] so much easier. Hell, they were dying up there—might as well! Everyone else on their ship was dead, they were alone on a dead ship thinking they were about to die, they might at least share a passionate kiss."

But it was not to be. Delenn pretends she didn't hear him, and although both know it has been said, they decide to ignore it . . . until three episodes down the line when it cannot be ignored any longer.

But it is Londo's fate that lies at the heart of this episode. His destiny has already been set. We saw him in the flashforward in "War without End" as a weak old man, an emperor in charge of a ravaged planet, and here we see how that comes about. "Londo has to redefine himself as emperor, which he doesn't particularly want to do," Joe explains. "He has a responsibility to be that person and to set aside his own personal considerations for his safety to carry out the role expected of him."

It was a big moment for actor Peter Jurasik, who had to make that final transition as Londo. "It was just such a grand story line with Centauri Prime coming down and Londo [being brought down], too. It truly was space opera time, big story line and mythic proportions and all that. Fun stuff to do."

Before he takes that final plunge to lead his people into a dark age under the ever-watchful eyes of the Drakh, he isolates himself from all those he cares about, partly to protect them and partly because this is a burden he has to carry alone. His first and most moving good-bye is to G'Kar. "It was a very powerful scene to do," Peter says. "It didn't feel perhaps to other people as if it was the end, but Andreas and I were both keenly and acutely aware that it was our last go around together, so it was a tough scene to do. In so many ways it was just a common and universal kind of experience for us. We had moments that we laughed through it, we had moments where we struggled to find the right beats, and so it had all the elements that made up what our relationship and our work together has been over the five years, and so it was the perfect one to end on."

"Because we were saying good-bye to each other as characters, and also as actors, as friends," Andreas Katsulas adds. "It was a good-bye on different levels, it was also a lot of gratitude and respect for each other, certainly from my side. Peter just made this a very good experience for me and pleasant to work with, so it was good-bye, old friend. It was very emotional."

It is perhaps a cliché for actors to talk about how wonderful it has been to work with another actor, but there is nothing but genuine feeling between these two who have played such impressive aliens on Babylon 5. Peter Jurasik even gets a little choked up as he talks about their final scene together. "Andreas is a fabulous actor all by himself and unto himself, but also with another actor. I speak about me. With his fellow actors he's incredibly generous and kind, and so many times we joked about the fact that he had to sit

and listen to what Joe Straczynski called a 'yak-yak speech.'
Andreas was so kind and giving to me, he really was. He
would be there for me over and over, and if you people who
watch the show, the dear fans, think that I get long-winded
and boring, you should try sitting across from me all day and
having to put up with it! He's a very generous man and it
touches me as a person, but also as an actor, how generous
Andreas has been with me and to me. So it was a sad scene
to have to do. He [Londo] doesn't know even what he wants
to say to him, he can't even find the words. Andreas' character, G'Kar, says, 'I understand,' and Londo says, 'I don't
know whether you really understand,' and in a sense Peter
feels that way about Andreas. I wish I could tell him how
wonderful it has been for five years, and the patience he has
shown and the kindness, but you can't. I can't. There's
nothing that I could put into words that could express that."

Having said his farewell to G'Kar, Londo is ready to
accept the hand that fate has dealt him or, more accurately,
what he has dealt himself in his earlier collaboration with
Morden and the Shadows. If it means that he has to accept
a keeper at his neck, then that is what he will do. "He is
completely blinded to any other actions than straight ahead
for the Centauri," Peter says. "I don't think he even realizes
what he's doing. He would do anything to protect his people.
That speech about 'We're going to rebuild and we're going
to isolate and come back,' even though he's being controlled
in a sense by the Drakh, there's so much that's quintessen-
tial in that speech. 'We'll come back and we'll rise up and we
don't need anybody else. I will now walk alone to my inauguration as a sign of my new isolationism.' Londo has just
thrown himself on the lover's cross for his people."

He dismisses Sheridan and the others in an officious
manner, unable to express his true feelings because of the
keeper controlling him, and the last image is of him sitting
alone on his throne. It is a sad end for one who was once
such a vibrant and fun-loving character.

19

"The Wheel of Fire"

Cast

President John Sheridan ....Bruce Boxleitner
Michael Garibaldi ....Jerry Doyle
Delenn ....Mira Furlan
Dr. Stephen Franklin ....Richard Biggs
Captain Elizabeth Lochley ....Tracy Scoggins
Zack Allan ....Jeff Conaway
Lyta Alexander ....Patricia Tallman
Londo Mollari ....Peter Jurasik
G'Kar ....Andreas Katsulas

Guest Stars

Officer ....Monique Edwards
Lise Hampton-Edgars ....Denise Gentile

The customs area is packed with Narns, eager to welcome G'Kar back from Centauri Prime. He stares at them in disbelief and horror, seeing images of himself on banners, pictures, and even statues. Uncertain what to say, he opens his mouth to speak, and they all kneel.

Garibaldi meanders embarrassingly through his report to the security council until Sheridan stops his slurred, unfocused speech. "You're drunk," he tells him, and Garibaldi cannot hide it any longer. Sheridan suspends Garibaldi from duty until he can sort out his problem.

Lochley finds Garibaldi wallowing in drunken self-pity in his room. She has come to tell him that she understands, that her father was an alcoholic, but Garibaldi scoffs and walks out. She follows him into the transport tube, reaching over to the control panel to stop it mid-journey. "I have the same exact damn problem," she says, and suddenly she has his attention. "I couldn't stop what was happening to my father, so I became the very thing I hated . . . If it could be swallowed, shot, or smoked, I did it." Lochley fights back her emotions and allows the tube to continue. "At least you know you're not alone," she finishes. "Everything else is up to you." The tube stops and Lochley walks out, leaving a quiet and thoughtful Garibaldi.

Lyta taps her fingers on the table of the Zocalo, looking defiantly at Lochley and the security team that have come to arrest her for allegedly buying weapons used to attack the Psi Corps back home. Gradually, everyone else joins in her tapping, all caught in a telepathic trance. Lyta regards Lochley with a superior stare. They can't arrest someone who has been touched by the Vorlons, she says. Then she senses a PPG aimed at the back of her head. "You're not the only one around here who's been touched by the Vorlons," Sheridan says, and she is forced to release the Zocalo from the trance. Lochley knocks her unconscious and the guards take her away.

Lochley shows Garibaldi into the customs area and there, in the milieu of disembarking people, he sees Lise. "I came as soon as I got your message," she says and runs toward him. As they embrace, he shoots a look to Lochley, who smiles. She was the one who sent the message.

"Bastards!" mutters Delenn, who's been talking to the Narn government about their threat to boycott all Alliance ships until G'Kar agrees to go home. As Franklin and Sheridan exchange shocked glances, she becomes dizzy. Sheridan rushes over to her, and she faints into his arms. Franklin examines her and confirms what he thought was almost impossible: Delenn is pregnant.

Lyta, strapped into a restraining jacket, regards Garibaldi as he enters her cell. He promises to get the charges against her dropped if she can remove the neural block implanted by Bester. But she wants more—for Garibaldi to set up a secret fund that can be used to hurt the Psi Corps and help rogue telepaths. Garibaldi agrees, but first he wants to know the truth about her increased abilities. She tells him she believes the Vorlons created

*her to be the ultimate weapon in their war against the
Shadows. When he confirms that she is a living
doomsday device, she opens her eyes and reveals a
glowing, Vorlon-white presence inside. "Pleased to meet
you, Mr. Garibaldi," it says.*

*G'Kar interrupts Garibaldi and Lochley with an
unexpected solution to the Lyta problem. He wants to
escape his people's attempts to turn him into a religious
icon and their attempts to get him to set up a new
government. What could be better, he suggests, than to
explore the galaxy with Lyta as his traveling companion.*

In every addict's life comes a time when he has to face up
to his addiction. For Garibaldi, that time comes during "The
Wheel of Fire." While friends like Zack were prepared to
help him cover up his drunkenness, he could deny that he
had a real problem. But after one drunken session too many,
turning up late and unprepared for a meeting, not able to get
himself into a state where he could even bluff his way
through, he cannot disguise his condition any longer. Sheridan tells him he is drunk and removes him from his job.

"That was great," Jerry Doyle, who plays Garibaldi, says.
"At one point in the scene I say to him, 'How long am I sus-
pended?' and he says, 'Until you work this all out.' In my
own moment I was thinking to myself, this could take a really
long time; I was almost saying, 'What if it takes too long?'
He just looked at me and said, 'It takes what it takes—I'll be
here,' and it just got me, man. It just hit me, it pulled my
heart. I just started tearing up and they went 'cut' on the
master shot and I went walking off. I was like 'Phew, I don't
know, I've got to think about this one.' So I went to Bruce
and I said, two leading guys sitting there getting misty-eyed,
is that going to work out? He said 'Yeah, you threw that line
at me, I don't know what was on it, but I hit it back over the
net and you got at it and it just happened.' Then when we
went in for the closeups, it still kept coming. I don't want to
say it was a scene about crying because when you watch
somebody cry, to me, it's really anticlimactic. I think to watch
someone trying not to cry or trying not to get emotional,

fighting it, is to me the more dramatic choice. At some point you're going to break down, but fighting it I think is that human element, you're trying to keep it down, you're trying not to let it all overcome you. It was a great scene, it was one of those ones. You get moments in this job where you connect on a deeper level than you do on others. We're just spitting a lot of scenes out, and sometimes they hit, and that one hit."

"It was about somebody confronting his alcoholism, and Sheridan, instead of dismissing him, after all the things that he's done to him, was quite forgiving of him," Bruce Boxleitner, who plays Sheridan, adds. "Maybe that's part of the change he's done with assuming the presidency, he's become much more compassionate in certain respects about his friends, not so judgmental. It was kind of a warm scene between the two of us, saying, 'I'll still be here when you go through all this, but you've got to go through it.' I didn't know if I, Bruce Boxleitner, was talking to Jerry Doyle. We've become so interwoven now, the four of us: Jerry, Garibaldi, John Sheridan, and me. But it was a very easy scene, very easy, and I liked that. I didn't have any technobabble, I didn't have any strategic, galactic stuff to say, it was just two people talking and that's where I think the really good drama happens."

Yet, even then, at the point of accepting that he screwed up, Garibaldi is not quite ready to pull himself out of the mire. He is just ready to wallow in self-pity. It is only a confrontation with Lochley, someone who isn't a friend, that begins to pull him out of it. "I don't think it was any one person," Jerry says. "I think it was a team effort, I think it was Bruce, and Tracy, and Denise, and Jeff, and Rick [Sheridan, Lochley, Lise, Zack, and Franklin], each in his own way saying, 'If you need anything, come talk to me.' All those people that in their own way contributed to Garibaldi getting his shit together, or at least facing it, and having that support group around, which was very important."

The sequence in which Lochley talks to Garibaldi about his addiction is another powerful moment in the episode. Although it is all directed at him, it reveals more about her.

We caught a glimpse of Lochley's troubled teenage years in "The Day of the Dead," and here she expands upon them, opening up herself just that little bit more. "There were some very telling things," actress Tracy Scoggins says. "Even little things that weren't that emotional. Even a sentence like 'When my mother died, I was the one that had to go through the house and decide what to keep and what to sell'—that speaks volumes right there. Whether there's brothers, sisters, uncles, aunts, Lochley was the one that was thrown into that position early on, and I think that really tells a lot about a person."

That was Janet Greek's last episode—although she returned at the end of the year to direct the *Babylon 5* TV movie *The River of Souls*—so she took the opportunity to say her own farewell to the series with some throwbacks to the first season. Remember those fresh oranges Sheridan raved about when he first arrived and that appeared prominently in "No Compromises"? Well, they're back. "In the very first scene when Garibaldi comes into the office, there's a big bowl of oranges in the office on the coffee table. I put them in a couple of shots so you clearly see the oranges," Janet says. "And in the first season, it was actually in Sinclair's office, but there were lots of scenes in that office where Garibaldi used to sit on the end of the desk. There's one in particular where I had Sinclair walk around and bring me to Jerry sitting on the desk. I did exactly that shot in this episode. It's after Lochley and Garibaldi's relationship is resolved—I have a scene where they're in the office talking. I put Garibaldi sitting on the edge of the desk just like he used to do and walked Lochley past him exactly the same way as an echo for the first season. I doubt anybody will realize that when they watch, except me, but it amused me to do it."

There are more revelations for Sheridan and Delenn when she discovers she is pregnant. It was a moment we knew was coming from the flash-forward in "War without End."

As a father of three boys, Bruce Boxleitner remembers what it is like to discover your wife is going to have a baby. "Great fear," he says. "There's an unknown there, and Mikey, our littlest one, it really was a frightening experience because we thought we might lose him and we could lose her, too. So I think I can relate to it pretty well. When you're a new father and mother, you have all kinds of fears come up because suddenly this other thing takes over, where you don't think so much about yourself anymore. It's amazing how that energy goes to this little child, and you're not so worried about certain things; the only thing you're worried about is whether you're going to be around long enough. But I think I can relate to Sheridan. I think there was a little fear, a little curiosity, what's it going to be? Then we have this fear when she's in the Medlab and the doctor was telling me and there were all these unknowns, we just didn't know. That would really plant fear into you."

Delenn's reaction is a mixture of emotions. She is surprised and happy, but there is also a hint of insecurity and fear. However, the description given in the script for the moment where Sheridan tells her the news, is a little unusual: "I leave her silent reaction, as they embrace, to Mira," it says.

"That was very sweet of him," actress Mira Furlan says. "I've never seen my name in those scripts throughout the five years. I've never seen my name on that paper in a *Babylon 5* script, so that was kind of a shocking thing to see those four letters in that context. A strange thing. It's nice to be so intimately addressed in a script."

Just as the season is approaching its end and story lines are concluding, others are being opened up. For Lyta, it is the transition into another phase. Her personal struggles are over, she has suppressed that side of herself, and now it is her power that is coming to the fore. She is so powerful that station Security feels the need to not only lock her in a cell, but also put her in a restraining jacket. "It's the sexiest straitjacket you've ever seen in your life!" Pat Tallman, who plays Lyta, says. "It just basically covers my shoulders and my arms and then fastens, of course, around the back. My arms are wrapped around me like a traditional straitjacket, but it's this really nice fabric, and it's open at the neckline, and when I put it on with the sweater that I had been wearing underneath my jacket, it became all about my cleavage—it was a different scene! So I went back to wardrobe and they pulled out a sweater that is the same texture and color, but it's cut a little higher, but it still had the same effect. I'm not a little woman, I'm a big girl and—not that I've got huge breasts or anything—but I have a full figure, and when your arms are under your boobs like that . . . it was just so funny! The crew loved it, the soundman loved it, everybody had a great time with that."

The final demonstration of what she has become is when she opens her eyes to Garibaldi and reveals the alien inside, glowing Vorlon-white. "I didn't understand that at all when I first read it; I had to talk to Joe about it," Pat says. "Evidently Lyta is a walking time bomb, a nuclear bomb ready to go off. She's got so much power in her, she can destroy everything. She destroyed Z'ha'dum, she's the one that did that. Okay, there are explosives on the planet, but she tripped it all. I think that's why he's sending me off into space, because with that kind of power what else can you do with the character except kill them or have them go away?"

20

"Objects in Motion"

Cast

President John Sheridan	Bruce Boxleitner
Michael Garibaldi	Jerry Doyle
Delenn	Mira Furlan
Dr. Stephen Franklin	Richard Biggs
Zack Allan	Jeff Conaway
Lyta Alexander	Patricia Tallman
G'Kar	Andreas Katsulas

Guest Stars

Lise Hampton-Edgars	Denise Gentile
Casey	James Hornbeck
Number One (Margaret Halloran)	Marjorie Monahan
Guard	Jeffrey James Castillo
Paretti	Walter Williamson
Tru'Nil	Neil Bradley

After throwing his guts up as part of his detox program, Garibaldi emerges from the bathroom to see Number One, the resistance leader from Mars, in his quarters. "In the next few days, someone is going to try and kill you," she says, looking round at Garibaldi and Lise. "Both of you."

"Whoa! Whoa!" Casey cries, running for the transport tube. The lone security guard inside holds the door for Casey to jump in. The guard stares into space as Casey chats away to him, then snick, *his eyes go wide in shock and pain. He slumps to the floor as Casey pulls a bloody knife out of his back. He rips the link off the guard's hand, replaces it with a fake, and leaves.*

G'Kar tries to step past one of his followers, but Tru'Nil, who is reverently clutching a statue of G'Kar, won't let him pass. "I made these for you," he says, offering G'Kar the statue. G'Kar looks aghast at the man responsible for spreading this iconography across the station, grabs the statue, snaps it in half, and strides off. Tru'Nil is furious.

A crowd has gathered in the Zocalo to see off G'Kar and Garibaldi—Zack's idea to smoke out Garibaldi's assassin. Zack knows the perp has a stolen link; at his signal, security throws a high-pitched squeal down the line. Casey flinches and yanks the earpiece out of his ear, and guards pile onto him. G'Kar steps forward to watch, as Tru'Nil emerges from the crowd. "G'Kar! You are not worthy of us!" he shouts, and pulls out a gun. Zack dives for G'Kar, knocking him out of the way just as Lise stands. Tru'Nil fires, the blast whizzing past G'Kar and striking Lise in the shoulder. "Lise!" Garibaldi says, cradling her unconscious body. "Lise!"

Garibaldi drags the struggling Casey into Lyta's cell. "Look in his head and tell me who sent him," he demands. With a thought, Lyta grips his mind and, as Garibaldi questions him, she plucks out the information. He was hired by the board of Edgars Industries, the Martian company owned by Lise.

Lise's eyes flutter open and she sees Garibaldi standing over her bed in Medlab. She's going to be okay. "We should get married. Right here, right now," he says. Taken aback, but delighted, she tells him to fetch the minister.

Guards bring Lyta to the docking bay where G'Kar's ship awaits her. With a glancing thought she throws off her restraints and joins her new Narn companion. "I find I'm actually looking forward to seeing the universe with you alongside, Lyta," he says. "It's going to be quite an adventure."

Garibaldi calls up Edgars Industries and faces the board over the StellarCom. He hits them with a whole list of blackmail material—illegitimate children, mistresses, a murder. Then he introduces them to Number One, the new head of covert intelligence for the Alliance, who discovered all of their little secrets. What's more, he tells them, he has set up a fund to pay handsomely for mercenaries to come after them if, for

any reason, he or Lise should die of unnatural causes.
The image of the board blips out, and Garibaldi turns
round, satisfied. He reaches for a bottle of booze,
unscrews the cap, and pours it down the sink. "I don't
need you anymore," he says with glee as it glugs away.
"What do you think about that!"

Franklin sits having dinner with Number One, or
Margaret Halloran as she can now be called. Of course,
with him going off to EarthDome and her working on
Babylon 5, they couldn't possibly conduct a relationship.
Although, Franklin does have an hour to spare before
his next shift . . .

On the face of it, "Objects in Motion" seems like another episode in which one of the main characters is threatened with assassination. We've seen them before in "Ceremonies of Light and Dark" and "No Compromises," to name two. But this one is cleverly done with the actual wounding shot coming not from Casey, the man hired by the board of Edgars Industries, as we expected, but from the G'Kar statue salesman, Tru'Nil. It's a nice piece of distraction that is introduced in what appears to be a stand-alone moment when G'Kar snaps one of Tru'Nil's masterpieces in two.

"Oh, I'm telling you, I think if someone who never saw our show saw one of these statues, they would want to buy one," Andreas Katsulas says. He was far more thrilled with the figures than his character was. "It's so well done, it's a work of art. It has a beautiful, total fidelity to the costume, every single inch of it is true and really captures something about G'Kar. Of course, it's very flattering, too, so that's why I love it so much! It portrays him as just so strong and noble and upright—it's really very well done." Andreas' reaction eventually prompted the official B5 Fan Club to begin selling limited edition replicas of the statues.

Back in the second season when a batch of Londo dolls were made for "There All the Honor Lies," Peter Jurasik was offered the chance to take one home with him as a souvenir. That didn't happen this time. "We weren't allowed to even breathe on them," Andreas says. "They had them all marked and security guards around them at all times. What they thought would happen, I don't know."

The actual assassination attempt, which is resolved relatively early on in the episode, is not really what the story is about. It is only a device to push other things into the open. One of those things is the relationship between Garibaldi and Lise. When she is injured, it brings into focus the fragile and unpredictable nature of life and provokes Garibaldi to ask her to marry him right there and then. "He's a rather impulsive character," actor Jerry Doyle admits, "so he proposes to her and decides to get married while she's lying shot and near death in Medlab. It's not exactly the most romantic of settings, but it's kind of the way he is."

The script called for Garibaldi to pop the question, tell Lise about the minister waiting to perform the ceremony just outside the door, and respond with a smile when Lise tells him to bring the minister in. When it came to filming the scene, Jerry Doyle decided to elaborate his performance. "It's such a heavy episode, there's a lot of good-byes, there's a lot of tears, there's a lot of emotion, and I just tried to make that scene with her a little lighter," he says. "She says, 'Tell him to get his ass in here,' which is so out of character for her, and then I'm like, 'Yeah? Yeah. *Yeah!*' So I go running down the end of the room, and I turn around and go, '*Yes!*' Then I go running out the door, and as I ran out of the door I had the director have an extra crossing the doorway as I left. I bumped into the extra, and I turned this guy into the camera. I look at him and go, 'I'm getting married!' and I kiss him, and then I go running off. I thought it would be a different way to approach that kind of a scene. Hopefully it cuts together well because this show is so heavy that it's going to need its lighter moments. You can only give the audience so much drama, then you've got to give them a break. You've got to throw a little bit of humor in there once in a while so they can go and have a laugh, then go back to crying."

More sexual relations are bubbling for Franklin. He's had a tough time with women over the five years—attracted to a patient who decided to go back to Earth in "The Long Dark," falling for a singer who died in "Walkabout," and then in the fourth season having to leave Number One behind on Mars. Now Number One is back and he gets to take another shot at it. "It's interesting," Franklin actor Richard Biggs says, "because we're not at war anymore, and I get to know her name and I get to try to figure out who she is and it's all in the pretense of knowing in a week I'll be gone. So that relationship seems to be doomed because if we're not in the middle of a war, or saving someone's life, or the whole planet, then when we do get together one of us is about ready to leave!"

The episode is, in many ways, about people. They are the "objects in motion," moving on from one part of their lives on Babylon 5 to new pastures. One of the strangest pairings in all this is G'Kar and Lyta, joining together to explore the galaxy. "I think it was a handy way to get him out of there and get her out of there and wrap up their stories," Andreas says. "I can certainly see that happening, G'Kar being that kind of person who thinks the way to serve his people is to write more about the universe. I think it leaves an upbeat feeling about G'Kar and Lyta. Their adventures: Will they become lovers? Will he become psychic? Will they have a psychic child? There's so much left to the imagination, it was a good way to wrap it up."

"Isn't that interesting?" Patricia Tallman, who plays Lyta, says. "I wouldn't have guessed that. We were joking when we rehearsed the scene. We were running our lines and I have a line where I say, 'I smell another book coming,' and Andreas turned round and said, 'I smell a spin-off!' It's from his mouth to Joe's ears."

Joe Straczynski does not deny it. "The best thing I can use is a *Lord of the Rings* analogy—and I know damn well everyone's going to go, 'Oh, he's going to that again!' After the war was over, the hobbits went off this way and the elves went off that way and Aragon went over there and the company began to break up. This is a similar situation. By the end of the season, a lot of our characters are scattered to the four winds, which in some ways makes them more accessible to me for *Crusade* and for any other outside projects. The crew is now gradually splintering off in different directions, following their own particular objectives." [*Dreamwatch*, issue 45]

The episode ends with Garibaldi's good-bye to Sheridan, Delenn, and the station. It is not quite his farewell to the show, but the same emotions were there, Jerry Doyle reveals: "They called for the liner and, as I looked to them, between them and just over their heads was the Babylon 5 docking bay sign. I looked at it and I was like, I'm really going. It's the end of the fifth season, I'm not talking to Sheridan and Delenn anymore, I'm talking to Bruce and Mira. And for some reason, it was a simple line of 'I gotta go,' and the hardest part was to say the line because I didn't want this to end. Even though we were shooting it the third day of a six-day shoot, to me it was still the last scene of leaving the station. Then Bruce came in and we were supposed to shake hands and something happened there and he said, 'Good luck to you,' and I said, 'You, too.' And then we broke, and they're still calling for the plane and I didn't want to go, and finally all I could get out at the end was a quiet 'Bye.'

"They yelled 'cut' on one of the takes on the master, and Lynn over in wardrobe was crying and everyone in makeup was crying. The DP, John Flinn, goes, 'Jesus, where do you want to go?' because we had to go into coverage [shooting from different angles to get closeups and so forth]. The way we were lit, logically, we would have shot it Bruce, Mira, me, then Denise [Gentile, Lise], but they were willing to flip the set around lightingwise in order to get to my closeup first because you're in that space. I said, 'No, I'm an actor,' and it was a good exercise to do a closeup and a medium closeup on Bruce, and have some takes on that, then on Mira, and then get around to me and still be able to find that place. I wanted to be able to work it to see what words were making it hit. We did Mira's closeup and her line was something like 'Of all the recent partings, I think this one will be the hardest.' I had my back to camera because I could just walk as far as the wall was, and I could just hear her, she just couldn't get the line out in her normal delivery. They yelled 'cut' and Bruce comes over and goes, 'Buddy, buddy, you're killing her, knock it off.' I was glad that I could give the same off camera that we tried to get on camera, because to me, acting is about reacting. It's what you're served that you volley back, and that was a good day of shooting. We got a lot of good stuff on film and I know that scene will cut together very nicely."

21
"Objects at Rest"

Cast

President John Sheridan	Bruce Boxleitner
Michael Garibaldi	Jerry Doyle
Delenn	Mira Furlan
Dr. Stephen Franklin	Richard Biggs
Captain Elizabeth Lochley	Tracy Scoggins
Lennier	Bill Mumy
Vir Cotto	Stephen Furst
Zack Allan	Jeff Conaway
Londo Mollari	Peter Jurasik
G'Kar	Andreas Katsulas

Guest Stars

Ta'Lon	Marshall Teague
Dr. Hobbs	Jennifer Balgobin
Ranger	Simon Billig
Lt. Corwin	Joshua Cox
Number One (Margaret Halloran)	Marjorie Monahan
ISN Reporter	Maggie Egan
Employee	Mike Manzoni

Ta'Lon enters G'Kar's quarters to find a message waiting for him. "Now that I am gone, someone else must speak for our people," G'Kar's image says. "I would like for that person to be you."

Dr. Hobbes looks nonplussed. She's just heard a similar thing from Dr. Franklin. "Good luck, Doctor," he tells her. "If you have any questions, you know where to find me." And with that, he walks off to the docking bay. He takes a last look around the place. "Bye . . ." he says simply, and heads for the ship that will take him to Earth.

Garibaldi strides into the boardroom of Edgars Industries on Mars, where a very nervous bunch of employees are seated around the table. He's their new

boss, and they look as if he's about to fire them for
previous transgressions. Actually, he's going to promote
them. They are to be his new board of directors.

The Central Corridor is packed with familiar faces.
Everyone, it seems, has gathered to see Sheridan and
Delenn leave. Delenn tells them there is no word for
good-bye in Minbari. In every parting there is a chance
of meeting again, so she does not say good-bye. "Our
souls are a part of this place, our hopes the foundation
of our future," she says. "We will pass this way again."

Lennier has arranged for Sheridan and Delenn to
command the White Star one last time, but as it heads
on automatic pilot for Minbar, Sheridan takes a walk to
ease his restlessness. He reacts at the sound of an alarm
and runs to where a Ranger is slumped by a tube leading
to the weapons system, gas leaking out all around him.
Sheridan tries to pull him clear. "No," the Ranger says.
"They're going to seal off the—" and a glass door slides
down, shutting them inside. Lennier comes racing
around a corner on the other side of the glass. Sheridan
calls to him, but Lennier hesitates. His rival for Delenn's
love is inside. He turns away.

Lennier, tormented at what he has done, turns back.
He runs into the hallway just as Sheridan has pried open
the door with the Ranger's fighting pike. A moment later,
Delenn runs round the corner to see Sheridan stagger to
safety and collapse. Lennier backs away in horror at his
own actions, finds a lone fighter, and heads as fast and as
far away as he can.

Sheridan, almost recovered from the gas, enters the
splendor of his new home with his wife, Delenn.
Sunlight streams in through the crystalline stained-glass
windows, each one representing a moment in Anla'shok
history. Sheridan steps out onto the balcony in the
twilight and, behind him, he hears a familiar voice:
Londo.

Londo's exuberance over dinner makes Sheridan and
Delenn ill at ease. He has come to give them a gift. Or
more accurately, an urn, which he asks them to pass on

to their child when he reaches adulthood. It is a Centauri tradition, he tells them, but that is a lie. Inside, a keeper lies dormant.

Sheridan cannot sleep. He has been thinking about his child and how he will not live to see him come of age. He sits alone in the dining room and records a message for his son's twenty-first birthday. He tells him to look to Delenn for wisdom and fire; to learn from his mistakes; that home is not a place, but where your passion takes you; to enjoy and remember your friends as life changes, and be willing to fight for what you believe. "Which brings me to the first piece of advice my dad ever gave me," he concludes. "Never start a fight, but always finish it."

The last *Babylon 5* episode ever. That simple fact had such an impact on the circumstances surrounding the filming of "Objects at Rest" that it forms its own subtext within the episode. Although it is not the last episode of the series—"Sleeping in Light," which remained in the can from the previous year's production, is that—it was the final one for cast and crew.

For J. Michael Straczynski it represented the culmination of ten years' work. From the genesis of the idea, through to the collaboration of many other talented hands and the uncertainties of cancellation or renewal, he kept the vision of his five-year story arc alive. Although *Babylon 5* was set to live on beyond those five years in spin-offs, movies, and reruns, "Objects at Rest" brought his original vision to a conclusion. At 4:54 A.M. on February 4, 1998, Joe Straczynski sat at his computer and composed the following message: "This was where it started. This is where it ends. Twenty minutes ago I finished writing the last episode we are going to shoot this year. Ten years of involvement, five years of production, 110 scripts total, 91 of them mine . . . All that led to that sentence. There are no words." [on the Internet]

The script is full of sentiments of farewell and reflection. And, although they come from the characters' mouths, many of them reflect back on the real lives of the real people involved. How telling it is that on the last page of the last script, Joe Straczynski, who has spent many long nights at the word processor, gives Sheridan the line, "I think I may even sleep in tomorrow" as he realized the prospect of reaching the end.

Whatever the feelings of the writer and the producers at completing the five-year story, they were compounded by the feelings of the actors when they actually came in to film the episode. No one knew at this stage if the spin-offs and movies that the producers were thinking about would involve them or indeed come to fruition. Even if they were involved, this was the last time they would experience *Babylon 5* in its original form. Bruce Boxleitner reflected during filming: "I find this is the saddest script. We're over Friday, we're done. And everything I'm saying in this particular story is like *me* saying it. What I have to say today, 'I've been so wracked with doubts . . .' and things, it's all these good-byes, and contemplating things and the past, and 'Did I do a good job?' It's like all these things the *actor* is saying."

Everyone was affected in a different way. Andreas Katsulas came in for one day to film G'Kar's message to Ta'Lon without any doubts at all. "I am so 'up' today and so full of energy and positive thoughts," he said that morning. "Just elated somehow at the thought that this has been five years and it's been such an incredible and wonderful thing to play G'Kar and with such a good group of people and everything. I am just so bubbly. I noticed that everyone around me is a little bit sad, and I feel conspicuous in my glee about it being the end and going on and doing other things. Of course, I'll be sad, I'll miss people, but there's no reason to miss them—I have a list of everyone's phone numbers, all I need to do is call them and say let's go out for a beer."

It was also a momentous occasion for the crew. Many would be staying to work on the *Babylon 5* spin-off *Crusade*, but not all. It certainly was an end of an era for them. To mark that, and as some kind of celebration, most of them make an appearance in this episode. Even most of the office staff were taken down to wardrobe, given something appropriate to wear, and put on the sound stage. You can spot designer John Iacovelli as one of Garibaldi's employees in the boardroom of Edgars Industries, while most of the crew appear in the Central Corridor to say their own farewell to Sheridan and Delenn.

Dr. Franklin's farewell, by contrast, was a much quieter affair, as actor Richard Biggs feels reflected the character. "I really felt that Stephen should just walk. Just walk, none of the looking back. No, the character's always looking forward, always looking ahead; he's already dealt with the relationships and said good-bye months ago; he's had a chance to really emotionally detach himself. Joe has written it that I come in, I tell the doctor that is taking my place, 'This is here, this is that, this is yours now, good-bye, good luck,' grab a bag, and I'm gone. And that's the character of Franklin."

But within all of these good-byes is also a story, revolving around the Drakh and the love triangle of Sheridan, Delenn, and Lennier. There had been a lot of preparation for this moment throughout the season. As early as "No Compromises" we saw Lennier's feelings for Delenn as he tells her he is leaving for the Rangers, and then, of course, there was his open declaration of his love in "The Fall of Centauri Prime." But even so, Bill Mumy felt uncomfortable about his character's final betrayal of Sheridan. "I've been wrestling with this particular script for a month now," he said during the filming of the episode.

The betrayal gives the episode a bittersweet ending. There is a sense of everyone walking off into the sunset, but it is tinged with these final acts that prove that a new beginning is not necessarily Utopia. Lennier's rash moment of selfishness proves that. But more ominously it is Londo's "gift" to Sheridan and Delenn's son that lays down trouble for the future. "I love what Joe has done with that final twist for him, of what the Drakh has him do," Londo actor Peter Jurasik says. "I feel Joe has ended up the character right where he should end up, not bending too much to sentiment. The leopard kept his spots to the end."

This episode was directed by the show's producer John Copeland, who took some of his cues from Jesús Treviño's direction of the previous episode, "Objects in Motion." Jesús tried to get a sense of all the characters moving through that episode, and John continues that visual theme in "Objects at Rest," except that he brings the characters to a stop. Sheridan is the only one to keep moving through the episode until, finally, he comes to rest on Minbar and delivers that moving speech to his unborn child.

"Yes, it's really beautiful," Bruce Boxleitner agrees. "That's where the show really shines, when you have dialogue like that. Plus, I can relate to it. I have three sons and I think I know how I would say these very same things if I knew I didn't have very long to live."

And that speech, looking forward to his death, sets the scene for Sheridan's final moments and "Sleeping in Light."

22
"Sleeping in Light"

Cast

President John Sheridan ....Bruce Boxleitner
Commander Susan Ivanova ....Claudia Christian
Michael Garibaldi ....Jerry Doyle
Delenn ....Mira Furlan
Dr. Stephen Franklin ....Richard Biggs
Vir Cotto ....Stephen Furst
Zack Allan ....Jeff Conaway

Guest Stars

Lorien (also flashback from #402 & #404) ....
....Wayne Alexander
Publicist ....Romy Rosemont
Commander Nils ....David Wells
Mary ....Sharon Annett
Aide ....Dan Sachoff
Ranger ....Lair Torrant
Captain of the Guard ....Kent Minault
Ambassador #2 (flashback from #403) ....
....William Scudder

*Twenty years after the Shadow War and the formation
of the Interstellar Alliance, and Sheridan lies sleeping on
Minbar, dreaming of Lorien, the being that once rescued
him from death. The First One, who gave some of
himself so that Sheridan might live, had said it would be
only enough to sustain Sheridan twenty years. Sheridan
wakes and goes into the garden to look at the predawn
beauty of the city of Tuzanor. His wife joins him and
takes his hand. "I'm almost out of time, Delenn," he
says. "But time enough . . ."*

*The door to Admiral Ivanova's office on EarthDome
bursts open and a guard comes flying through it. The
Ranger who hit him steps inside, followed by Ivanova's
flustered aide apologizing for the intrusion and*

muttering something about protocol. Ivanova scowls at her aide and takes a message from the Ranger's hand. "Tell him," she says to the Ranger, her voice quiet and reflective, "I'm on my way."

The sound of giggling emerges from under the covers of Emperor Vir Cotto's bed, but is halted by a knock at the door. Vir gets out of bed as two Centauri women scuttle out of the room. He looks at the Ranger standing there and takes a message from his hand.

Sixteen-year-old Mary Garibaldi enters the solarium at the Edgars estate all fired up from a tennis game with Dr. Franklin, who looks beat. Her father looks up from his paper and promises to show her how the game should be played. But moments after heading off to the court, she's back, looking slightly worried. A Ranger has arrived at their house with a message.

They all gather on Minbar for one last dinner party. They reminisce about old times, their laughter ultimately tinged with sadness. Sheridan proposes a toast to absent friends and they remember: G'Kar . . . Londo . . . Lennier . . . Marcus.

The following day, before the others are awake, Sheridan takes out his black uniform for a final tour of duty. Delenn greets him, and they know this will be the last time they will see each other. They fight back tears and embrace. "Good night, my love, the brightest star in the sky," Sheridan says. "Good night, you have been my sky and my sun and my moon," Delenn says. And eventually, reluctantly, they pull away. He heads out toward the waiting ship without looking back.

Sheridan stops off at Babylon 5 one last time. The space station, like him, is almost at the end of its time. Redundant and in the process of being decommissioned, it is almost empty, apart from the echoes of times past, of battles fought and won, and of people long since moved on.

Sheridan's mind returns to the present and he sees Zack, a little older, with a slight limp, watching him listen to the echoes. "We changed the world," Zack

reflects. "We did everything we said we were gonna do.
And nobody can take that away from us. Or this place."
A sudden dizzy spell passes over Sheridan and he puts
out his hand to steady himself against the wall. Time to
move on.

A jump-point opens in the Coriana system, where they
won the Shadow War, and Sheridan's ship enters normal
space. He holds position, staring out at the stars until a
faint blue-white light forms outside his ship, shimmering
into the ghostly shape of Lorien. "Who are you? . . .
What do you want? . . . Why are you here? . . . Where
are you going?" Lorien, his voice coming from the void
says. Lorien has been waiting for Sheridan, for the time
he would return to the End of the Beginning, to go
beyond the Rim and begin a new journey. A soft white
light slowly surrounds Sheridan. He stops breathing, and
in that moment of stillness, the light intensifies until it
engulfs him completely.

The last maintenance man leaves Babylon 5, turning
out the light as he goes. The last shuttle departs, and
from within the station's core comes a deep rumble. A
series of explosions blast along its length until it is
consumed in fire.

On Minbar, Ivanova dons her new robes to take the
position as head of the Rangers, and Delenn watches the
sun rise across Tuzanor. As for Sheridan, his ship was
retrieved from the Coriana system, but his body was
never found.

What can be said about "Sleeping in Light" that isn't already on the screen? It is a deeply moving tribute to the show's five-year history, with a sense of reflection and overwhelming sadness as the destruction of the Babylon 5 space station and the death of Sheridan bring the phenomenal series to a close.

J. Michael Straczynski has said that writing a script involves going through what the characters go through. Writing "Sleeping in Light" was therefore just as an emotional experience for him as it was for the people in the story. "I lost it several times as I was writing it, due to the content," he admits. "There's one scene in particular, you'll know when you see it, that put me away for an hour when I finished writing it."

Even on paper it was incredibly powerful. Mira Furlan remembers, "It just brought tears to my eyes when I read it." Richard Biggs was similarly moved: "Laurie [his then-fiancé and now wife] and I were in Palm Springs, and I was reading the script for the first time. I remember just feeling sad about what I was reading. It was a really beautiful script."

For such a landmark episode, Joe Straczynski decided to do what he had never done before and direct it himself. It meant that he was there at every moment, making sure the exact vision he had in his head was translated onto the screen. He hoped, too, that this experience would help him become a better writer.

It was also a chance for the actors to gain more insight into the workings of Joe's mind, get closer to the creator of the words, and joke about seeing him up so early in the morning. "It's funny," Rick Biggs comments, "because the directors have to get up at six in the morning and Joe's not a morning person. So it was interesting to come to the set and say [in a bright and breezy manner] 'Hi, Joe!' [and have him reply] 'Urrrrh . . .' I think it was real helpful to have the guy who wrote it, is producing it, there directing. There's nobody that knows the script better than him, so when he leans over and whispers something in your ear, you definitely know that's where you should go."

"I really don't know if I'd say that I *enjoyed* it," Joe commented soon after he had completed the episode. "My main concern every day was somehow getting through it without embarrassing myself, or letting down the crew or the cast or, ultimately, the viewers. I wanted the direction to be equal to the performances I knew were waiting to be unlocked. [on the Internet]

"[But] I blew [it] on the very first day. The very first shot, they're ready to go through the first rehearsal, and I'm watching through the monitor, and my first AD leans over to me and says, 'You have to say "action" or they can't move!' "

With the story set almost twenty years into the future, the cast had to spend a little bit longer in the makeup chair each morning. According to some, it is not exactly a flattering prospect to look in the mirror and find an older person looking back at you. "I had a lot of latex aging around the eyes to make myself have wrinkles. I didn't like that at all," Stephen Furst, who played an old Emperor Vir, says. "I went, 'God, I am not a handsome older man, I am not growing old with grace.' "

Jeff Conaway, who plays Zack, had a similar reaction. "I was complaining that they aged me too much. Zack and his vanity! Everybody else looked great, I looked like I'd gone through a meat grinder or something. They eventually toned it down some because it was so craggy and wrinkled, I'm like, 'Come on, it's twenty years, not forty years.' "

"They had tried to put on a fake beard and mustache, and when I walked on the set, I looked like Wilford Brimley [the actor]," Garibaldi actor Jerry Doyle says. "I just said 'No, this ain't cutting it, guys.' I did a makeup test a week before we shot it—they had used a little shrink stuff right behind the eyes and they had made me up and I looked pretty Orwellian. I said 'No, I'm not going to look like this when I'm sixty; I look too big, too old. I'm married to this girl Lise, and you think she's going to be married to some guy like this?' I said, 'This is how I think it should be twenty years from now.' We worked on it, had two or three makeup tests, and then we got it to a point that I think is believable. And Joe was very nice, he let me smoke a cigar in the final episode, so now I can deduct my cigar expenses as a prop expense! Seeing as I am now the richest man in the universe, with the sexiest woman in the universe, why not sit there, read the paper, and smoke a cigar?"

It is a very satisfactory end for many of the characters. Garibaldi may have gone to hell and back, but he has found contentment with a conventional home life. Franklin is as he has always been, except now he has the whole resources of EarthDome in which to indulge his passion in xenobiology. It did not end well for everyone—Marcus, we know, died to save Ivanova; Lennier is dead; and Londo and G'Kar died with their hands around each other's throats, as we know from both the flash-forward in "War without End" and Londo's prophetic dream. But for those who survived, life has treated them well. "I have a scene with two Centauri women," Stephen Furst says. "So it ended fine for me!"

The only one who seems at odds with her life is Ivanova, still harboring guilt for Marcus' death. She has been promoted to Admiral, but shows none of the contentment of Garibaldi or Franklin. Instead she seems at odds with her job, if not her whole existence. Ivanova only makes an appearance in this episode because it was filmed at the end of the fourth season when Claudia Christian was still on the show. "I quite liked playing her as a curmudgeonly old Janet Reno [the U.S. attorney general] bulldog," she said soon afterwards. "She's sick of her job, she feels like she's just an old war horse, so that was enjoyable. I got to be even more trollish and troglodytish and curmudgeonly than I normally am." It is suggested that her new job, heading the Rangers, may give her a new purpose and, indeed, carry on the work that Sheridan and Delenn started.

It is the Sheridan and Delenn story that holds the real power here, as we see an older Sheridan on the point of death. "I really grew the beard out, put white in my hair, and my beard was much longer—I looked like Ulysses S. Grant," actor Bruce Boxleitner says. "I was out of uniform and wore Minbari clothing; I felt much more medieval in a way. Now I know how they feel, they walk around more like in a Shakespearean play. I really tried to move much older, even though he's not, he's only in his mid-sixties. I just tried to play a much more at peace man, much wiser, much more thoughtful about everything and accepting of his fate and it was time to pay the piper. That was very sad. I used Sean Connery in *First Knight* as my idea, the older King Arthur."

The sadness was intensified by the uncertainties surrounding the show at the time. It was 1997 and it seemed that *Babylon 5* would not be renewed for another season. "Sleeping in Light" was designed to be the last episode, whether the show ran for four or five years, and it looked increasingly likely that the dream of a five-year story would be shattered. All this added to the emotion on the set, giving many of the key scenes an added charge. "We had a lot of sniffling going on," Bruce remembers. "All the girls from the office were sitting there watching us. We wanted it to be really more romantic in that great way that older people are romantic, not hot sexual, just knowing and caring and both of us very familiar with each other. Completing each other's sentences, reading each other's thoughts. I think both Mira and I enjoyed playing those roles. Very sad, especially on our last good-bye. That was a tough one. Overdramatic as hell, but fun. I'm never afraid to be sentimental. I think people want sentimentality, I really do. I think in those kind of scenes, if you're going to play them, play them, don't be afraid."

"When we did it, it was a strange experience," Mira Furlan, who plays Delenn, remembers. "It's not only how it's written and what we're playing, which is incredibly sad, but also it was the end of the whole series. We were all together with the whole crew, we were all in tears constantly. Bruce and I, there were moments when we had to wait until we calmed down and could say the lines."

Then, Sheridan makes his final visit to Babylon 5, seeing it ready to be demolished at the end of its life, and it's another moment that tugs at the heartstrings. Richard Biggs found the whole atmosphere very strange. "I remember seeing they had cleaned out the Zocalo. There we all were, and we all looked a little older, and there was the feeling that this might be the last time that we ever saw Babylon 5, in the script and in real life. So it's real easy to connect as you look over and you see someone you've worked with for four years, and look up and see the Zocalo, and know that this could be the last time you're going to see it."

"It was great, but kind of sad," Bruce says. "I know [executive producer] Doug Netter walked up to me later and said, 'It was very hard, Bruce, very hard to watch. You were all of us there, you were doing it for all of us, that last look around.' And it was very difficult for Joe because, really, we all thought this was it."

But there is a positive end to the episode and to the

series. Sheridan's death is merely a journey toward a different form of existence beyond the Rim. It ends on an uplifting note of achievement. Babylon 5 was our last, best hope for peace, and despite interstellar wars and internal struggles, it managed to fulfill its dream. The subtext lying under all of this is the achievement of the show itself, of fulfilling its goal to tell a five-year story.

The end of "Sleeping in Light" is not the end of *Babylon 5*. After it was filmed, the long-sought-after commission for a fifth season came through, and after it was completed, a follow-up series began production. But it is a full stop in the five-year journey, one that has completed its tale and is ready to make way for others that may follow.

ANNOUNCING THE PAST, PRESENT AND FUTURE OF...

ALL NEW EPISODES
BABYLON 5: THE FIFTH SEASON
WEDNESDAYS 8PM (ET)

THE SERIES: SEASONS 1–4
BABYLON 5
MONDAYS-FRIDAYS